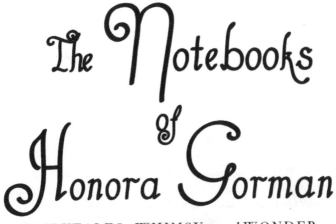

The Notebooks of Honora Gorman

FAIRYTALES, WHIMSY, *and* WONDER

LINDA MAHKOVEC

Design and distribution by Bublish, Inc.

ISBN: 978-1-647046-11-8 (paperback)
ISBN: 978-1-647046-10-1 (eBook)

Other Books by Linda Mahkovec

The Garden House

And So We Dream

The Christmastime Series

Christmastime 1939: Prequel to the Christmastime Series

Christmastime 1940: A Love Story

Christmastime 1941: A Love Story

Christmastime 1942: A Love Story

Christmastime 1943: A Love Story

Christmastime 1944: A Love Story

Christmastime 1945: A Love Story

Short Collections

The Dreams of Youth

Seven Tales of Love

NOTEBOOK 1

(Somewhere in the 1980s)

Call it escapism, if you will. Honora glanced at her watch, whipped off her white apron, and tucked it beneath the waiters' station. Time to flee.

The other waiters eyed her as they gathered around the staff lunch to chat, gossip, complain, and joke, slipping into their true actor/artist personas – crossing legs, waving cigarettes around, discussing auditions. They likened her to a particular cartoon character who always exited so quickly that her hairpins flew out (a cackling witch, if memory served Honora correctly).

"Where's the fire? Slow down, Honey!" It amused the head waiter to shorten her name to Honey or Nora when taunting her. Little did he know that Honey and Nora were already two distinct (and often contentious) sides to her.

"Come, on! No leftover pasta for you?" a waitress called out.

"Not today. See you soon!"

Honora grabbed her bag, pushed open the restaurant door, and greeted the streets of Manhattan with a deep inhale and a smile. Although she was marked as a waiter – black pants, black shoes, white shirt, black suspenders – she felt confident that the thin, pale-blue tie (from a vintage clothing store) and small pearl drop earrings softened the waiter's attire and perhaps suggested that she was an artist. Of some sort, anyway. This was New York, after all!

She turned to the left for a change, assuming a café would be easy to find. But the closer she got to Fifth Avenue, the more crowded (and expensive) the posted menus became. So, she backtracked to a little lunch place she had been to before. She stepped inside and took a seat at a small table near the window that was just being reset.

The clock showed that she had two hours before the dinner shift. Enough time to work on her children's story for class. She pulled out a beautiful, thick notebook. The cover was patterned in deep rich colors, suggestive of Moroccan tiles – midnight blue, dusty magenta, peacock – and bordered in gold filigree. (Honey was dazzled by its beauty.) Rather large and heavy, but then Honora had a lot to say.

New beginnings required new notebooks. Formal notebooks. Not the countless spirals and notepads of all sizes, including those small enough to tuck into a purse or pocket should inspiration strike. Not to mention the myriad scraps, napkins, post-its, backs of envelopes, inside book covers (front and back), and all the other places Honora had jotted down ideas and impressions over the years. Scenes, descriptions, snippets of conversations, odd pairings of words, the way a person cupped a chin in thought, or walked in a manner that caught her attention, or the beauty of an unusual sunset sky. All her attempts to capture the elusive world.

One of Honora's treasures was a small wooden chest, handsome and exotic, with Chinese characters, antique looking with brass hinges. She filled it with her miscellaneous scraps of writings over the years (the smallest entries on business cards from stores, matchbook covers from restaurants, and even on the backs of fortune cookie slips). At some point in the future, she would sort them and make sense of it all, categorize everything, use parts to form stories.

Though there were times when that mess of scribbling was too much for her poor brain and she came close to chucking the whole thing out the window. What held her back? Possibility. What if – on one scrap of paper was the line that would launch the book that would become her masterpiece? And so, she kept filling the wooden chest with scraps of writing.

She also had a somewhat more organized collection: notepads for her schoolwork, diaries for her love life, and journals for the day to day, family visits and vacations. And there was a very slim folder for her poetry (she knew she was no good at it, but if she could file a description of someone who walked as if they had an extra joint in their legs, then surely she could file away her poems).

And now, there were the Notebooks. The Notebooks! For the time – at long last – had arrived. Honora had completed her degree (that would one day lead to a *career* – a word with prison bars around it, along with *corporate world, workforce, 9-5* . . .) and moved to the writing and publishing capital of the world.

After years of planning, dreaming, scraping, and saving, she had turned away from a past too full of yearning, and was ready to begin. Now was the time to write. To create worlds, explore strange lands, step into the lives of marvelous characters, and finally live the life she had always dreamed about.

The Notebooks would chronicle the writer's life, the artist's life. Or at least her attempt to live such a life. She would include a few finished pieces from her writing classes. Children's stories. Short stories. Possibly notes for a screenplay, ideas for a novel or two, down the road. The Notebooks held the part of her life that was blissfully, thrillingly flung wide open.

After Honora had found a job and a room to rent in Manhattan, she took the subway to the Christopher Street station, strolled through the Village, and stopped at a small stationery shop. She bought the beautiful notebook to fill with her impressions of this most wondrous city. Her steps took her to MacDougal Street, and another discovery – the tiny coffee shop called Caffe Reggio. She sat at a round, richly carved table, and took in the chamber music filling the air, the dark Italianate paintings, the scent of coffee, the hiss of cappuccinos being made. She overheard a discussion about a theater production, and noted other writers tucked into corners, absorbed in their worlds. Her soul breathed in all that loveliness and hope and excitement. And her beautiful new notebook mirrored all that.

She had opened the notebook, lifted her pen – and froze. Maybe she should have purchased a plain old spiral notebook. She hated to mess up this pretty one. What if what she had to say was stupid, what if she scratched it out, what if – (the authoritative Nora gave her a sharp elbow to the side. *"Pick up that pen and write something. Anything!"*). Honora had smoothed down the page, and wrote on the top line: *Book the First*. A thrill shot through her.

With pen poised above the white page, she wrote her first entry: I come from a long line of women.

She nodded, took a sip of cappuccino, and looked up at the paintings, thinking of her mother, her grandmother, Jane Eyre and Mrs. Dalloway, Colette and George Eliot, as well as some of her creations on the scraps of papers. She added the words: real, fictional, and in the process of being made up. *Yes*, she thought. *That about sums me up.* She added an emphatic period after the line and smiled. *Now, let's begin.*

That had been nearly a year ago. Now, on her lunch break from her waitressing job, Honora sat at one of those tiny squeezed-in cafés on the side streets of Manhattan and browsed the menu. She pretended not to notice the puzzled brow of the waiter who cocked his head at her waiter's uniform.

"I'll have the quiche and a cup of tea," she said, with a firm Nora-like nod. *There go my lunch earnings.* She could always pick up additional shifts to meet the rent. This was important.

She smiled at the phrase, "Book the First," that had flowed so effortlessly from her pen. Not the more prosaic, "Book 1." She had an uncle who spoke like that, in a playful nineteenth-century literary manner. That's how he began his letters to her: "Page the first. Now then, I take pen in hand and write . . ." He was a great reader, a great traveler (154 countries to date), and altogether delightfully eccentric. Some of his ways had rubbed off on her over the years.

A draft of her children's story was due soon. Honora read over the instructions for the assignment, lifted her pen, and waited for inspiration to strike. (*"It doesn't work that way!"* she heard Nora say.) *I know, I know.*

She stirred sugar into her tea, and glanced at a few early entries. Perhaps they would contain a phrase or image that would spark a story idea. She loved those first early pages.

How thrilled she had been to finally be here. True, New York City was expensive, and difficult in some ways. But she had found the waitressing job through a friend in a playwriting class, and it would do until she found something else. A job better suited to an English major with a minor in creative writing. (She ignored the sarcastic chuckle from Nora.)

Those first weeks and months had been full of open-mouthed, wide-eyed wonder, even when she was just exploring her neighborhood. Every street, every corner held astonishing sights and sounds. Something as simple as the street vendors had caused her amazement and evoked a sense of discovery – shawls and long, fluttering skirts (she now had several), incense, books, handmade cards, jewelry, frames, hats, original artwork, and of course the tourist items: miniature Empire State Buildings, NYC-themed caps, green foam Statue of Liberty crowns, Broadway-inspired *Phantom of the Opera* masks, *Cats* T-shirts and bags . . . The variety was a wonder to behold.

Another simple yet delightful surprise was the singing. There was more singing in New York City – people walking down the sidewalks, not just humming to themselves, but belting out a song. If they had stopped and held out a hat, people would have listened and given coins. From open windows poured scales, arias, and show tunes. Was it the nearness to Broadway and Carnegie Hall and Julliard? Or was singing woven into the whole city?

Everything was so new, so different. A walk down any given street would be full of hurrying people speaking languages she couldn't even guess at. People of all kinds, all manner of dress, all colors of skin, all styles of hair. A mini-world. Amazements large and small.

Like the muscular, man-with-a mission bicyclist who flew past her on busy Eighth Avenue. She had tipped her head in confusion at the crutch strapped to his bike – and gasped when she saw that he had only one leg. That didn't stop him. Probably nothing was ever going to stop him. She had the impression that people tried harder here in this whirlwind, full-tilt city.

Then there was the gypsy family who lived on the first floor of her apartment building. She had been fascinated by the grandmother who told fortunes and the three little sisters with big eyes and long dark hair, so similar in appearance that they looked like the same girl at different ages – four, six, eight. The night of the terrible screaming when the father and "patriarch" died of a heart attack. And how after that, they were gone. Vanished. Like in that poem: they "fold their tents, like the Arabs, And as silently steal away." She hadn't seen or heard them moving away, but days soon after, the sign outside the stoop – "Card Reader / Palm Reader, First Floor" – was in the trash. The plaque on their door, "Mrs. Ana, Card reader," was gone, leaving a small rectangular emptiness.

Perhaps the most astounding amazement happened one morning in her first place, a room on Ninth Avenue. She had gotten used to the late-night clip-clopping of the Central Park carriage horses being returned to the stables. And though she had been initially surprised, and delighted, by the unexpected, old-fashioned sound (which sometimes triggered storylines as she drifted off to sleep), it soon became just another rich detail of the fascinating city. However, the horses passing outside her window at night did not prepare her for what she saw one morning. Honora had been awakened by absolute quiet – no sirens, no cars honking, no buses whishing, or people talking/yelling/singing. Just silence. Not a Ninth Avenue sound, ever. She had risen from her bed, parted the curtains, and gaped! There below, marching along in slow procession, she saw – ELEPHANTS! She was tempted to do a cartoon-like fisted rubbing of her eyes. This can't be possible! There can't be elephants outside my window in New York City. But there they were. She was later told they were part of the Annual Ringling Bros. Elephant Walk. Of course. (By the time she saw camels, donkeys, and sheep on a Midtown street – part of the *Christmas Show* at Rockefeller Center – she didn't even bat an eye.)

Then there was the afternoon she left the Metropolitan Museum of Art, cut through Central Park, and decided to start walking west to see how far she could get in this megacity. Only to be dumbfounded when, after just a few avenues, she saw the Hudson River, with New Jersey on the other side! Her sense of space had been shaped in her youth by the wide prairie lands of the Midwest, and so she had been astonished by the smallness of one of the greatest cities on earth. It was walkable!

The Metropolitan Museum itself was like a jaunt through history. In addition to standing in awe of the masterpieces she had studied in art classes, she had been captivated by the larger exhibits: the Spanish courtyard, the Japanese garden, the early American house. The Temple of Dendur! And the entire Egyptian section. It would take her years to explore the museum.

And the American Museum of Natural History – another world awaiting discovery. Animal dioramas, early peoples, totem poles and canoes, the planetarium, the suspended blue whale, the dinosaurs. The immensity and diversity of the universe was almost dizzying. The mineral and gem collection (Honey's favorite) brought it down to a smaller scale, an intimate room of natural beauty. (Nora had been more taken with the hanging solar system and the meteorites.)

There were countless smaller museums to visit, as well as all the neighborhoods and stores that made her feel as if she were traveling. Chinatown and Little Italy, shops that sold Tibetan brass singing bowls, Old Europe vintage postcards, Turkish painted pottery, French handcrafted soaps and candles. Ethnic cuisines that sometimes scented an entire block: Afghan, Ethiopian, Indian, Greek, Thai . . . The sounds and smells of a mini-world market.

Even the sky was different. There was less of it, for one thing. Honora missed the wide openness of Midwestern and Western skies and began to search for it in the city. It meant a lot of neck craning, since the tall buildings blocked out much of it. And there was no stargazing at night. Yet sometimes she would stop in wonder at the colors of the sunset sky over the Hudson River, or pause to gape at the sinking sun poised between the canyons of skyscrapers – a ball of orange perfectly positioned. (She was later to learn that on solstice days, people would refer to this spectacle as "Manhattanhenge." Just another simple wonder on the streets of New York City.)

Though Honora missed the stars, the lights of the city at night made up for it. She loved the contrast between the workaday gray of Manhattan and the magical, sparkling nights. The city, especially when viewed from afar, shone like a glittering firmament. A reversal of sorts, as if the starry night sky had been flipped to earth.

She would never forget her first arrival, approaching the massive metropolis at night – entranced by the wide expanse of twinkly lights, a galaxy of stars that stretched as far as she could see. It could be Fairyland, a futuristic city, or the exciting crossroads of the world, as it actually is. It beckons and allures, promising the best of everything, encouraging dreams into reality.

Honora's quiche arrived as she turned a page and read an early (Honey-inspired) strategy for the Notebooks: enter the best parts, the dream parts, the beauty parts, the wishful parts. All the rest belonged in the spirals, or in the Chinese chest, or would get wadded up and tossed. She wanted her notebooks to be filled with beauty and wonder and the best that she could be. Not the failures and the years of longing and disappointments, and – (*"Halt!"* cried Nora the enforcer. *"Wrong notebook."*) Honora gave a nod. It was so easy to slip into all that.

As she ate her quiche and salad, she continued to read the early entries.

"If I'm vague, it's because words are vague and what I mean is so precise." – HG (Honora was not above quoting herself.)

A Saturday morning. The tree leaves outside my kitchen window flutter mobile-like in the breeze. Shifting patterns. The trees play with the sunlight, taking it now, hiding it under its leaves. Few sounds. A broom sweeping in the courtyard below, the distant city hum, and that scent. A tree or plant? No, an old-time fragrance. I turned my face to the open window, perplexed by the scent – myrrh or frankincense? Ah – it was coming from the Greek Orthodox Church next door, wafting up into my kitchen window. A little surprise gift. I raised the sash higher and took it all in. Faint chanting, tiny bells, and incense. Of all things.

Honora smiled, remembering that moment of subtle wonder. Now she passed the church every day. Once in a while, the door stood open and she peered inside from the sidewalk – it glittered with candles and lamps and Byzantine beauty. St. George's Greek Orthodox Church. One of those pretty little churches that were wedged in between apartment buildings and businesses, all over Manhattan. Often, when she came across them, she stepped inside, always surprised to find these jewel-like mini-museums nearly empty. Full of artwork and wood carving, fragrances, and cool hushed air. She flipped forward a few pages to read her notes on another neighborhood gem, the Actor's Chapel. She clearly remembered that day.

"St. Malachy's." Close to the restaurant where she worked, not far from her apartment building. She had stumbled upon the church, and loved to occasionally visit it. The colors of ivory, old gold, warm burgundy, arched intimately over her, the statues, some white and simple, others ornate and glittering. She sat in a pew and glanced around her. There were only a few other people – two praying, one napping.

To her left, she overheard words and observed a little old lady dressed in a navy suit, a prim hat, a small handbag slipped over her wrist. She stood near the statues and votive candles, speaking out loud; conversing, actually.

Intrigued, Honora moved to the other end of the pew so that she could hear what the woman what saying.

"Oh, you fill me with joy, you, who gave to us your only son. Thank you. Here's a nickel." (Clink went the coin as she dropped it in the slot by the candles).

"You, who make me strong, save the homeless in our city. Here's a dime."

The little lady lit a candle. "Let this candle's flame be a token of my everlasting love. Here's another nickel."

In the middle of expressing her devotion, she fed her coins, bringing about who knew what goodness to the city.

Honora turned her head, as if almost catching the memory's subtle church scent – all holy and musty and sacred and ethereal. Oh, those sweet, early days.

She finished her quiche and paid the bill. The class assignment won't get written this way, she thought. Discipline!

But the truth was, she was stumped. The main character was supposed to search for something, and though

Honora had a little girl in mind and could envision her on an adventuresome quest, she didn't know what the little girl was searching for. A rough draft was due soon. A glance at the time told her she needed to get back to work in order to set up for dinner. She shut the notebook and tucked it into her bag.

Honora hurried back down 56th Street, pondering her character. A vague notion from her notebook had stuck in her mind. Something had sparked a germ of an idea. What was it – Elephants? Gypsies? Incense?

As she dodged pedestrians and deliveries, an old memory surfaced from when she was a little girl, four or five years old. An insignificant event and yet deep-rooted. She had found a tiny flat rock in the front yard, near the driveway. About the size of her thumbnail, with concentric circles. It had struck her as beautiful and filled her with delight. She had tossed it up into the sunlight, again and again. And then – it disappeared into the grass, never to be found again. And she had felt a deep sense of loss.

Honora felt a storyline emerging.

She entered the restaurant, tied on her apron, and began folding napkins in the waiters' station. The head waiter leaned against the counter next to her, working a crossword puzzle.

What was that seedling trying to root in her story – something about the sky? The night sky. And how she missed it. Stars! She flooded with inspiration. (Honey smiled. *"See, Nora? Sometimes musing does work."* Nora stood firm. *"Musing and waiting for the muse are two different things!"*)

Honora's hands stopped mid-fold and she looked up at the ceiling. "A falling star!" she said aloud and felt that deep bong of satisfaction when an idea resonated.

"Talking to yourself?" The head waiter had an amazing way of delivering the simplest utterances like foil thrusts. Slash! Scratch! Touché!

"Afraid so." She stacked the napkins and began to leave. She would give the tables in her station a quick check.

"Before you go – what's the capital of Guam? Five letters, third letter A."

"Agana," Honora answered, without missing that proverbial beat.

He knitted his eyebrows and penciled it in. "Huh. It works. Thank you, Magoo!" (his other nickname for her).

But Honora was already gone, thanking her world-traveling uncle for the postcards he had sent from his teaching stint in Guam.

Magoo! she thought. What was it with the head waiter and cartoons? And to think that he had gone to Yale. And spent a semester at Oxford! At a recent waiters' lunch, he had asked the question from an article he was reading: "What cartoon character are you most like?"

The responses flowed from the waiters: "Superman – no, probably more like Underdog." "Johnny Quest." "Snow White – before the apple. When she was hanging around with the dwarfs." "Scooby-Doo."

"Bugs, for me," said the head waiter. "I've always been a smartass." He turned to Honora and arched one eyebrow. "Let me guess – Cinderella."

"Wrong," she answered. "Mr. Magoo."

"Who?"

"I remember him!" said one of the older waiters. "He was this cheerful, half-blind old guy who always just missed disaster wherever he went – stepping onto an I-beam that a crane was lifting, driving onto a roller coaster and just missing a collision as he veered off onto telephone wires. Completely oblivious. But he always ended up at his destination. Chuckling along the way, tipping his hat courteously to strangers." The waiter turned to Honora. "But *you* – Magoo? Noooo." He tilted his head. "You'd make a good Cinderella."

Honora feared it was the scullery maid version, not the princess. After all, here she was, bussing tables, polishing silverware, taking orders.

At least they hadn't brought up the speedy, hair-pinned witch. Like Mr. Magoo, Honora believed that despite all the detours, surprise roads, dead ends, missteps and completely wrong career paths – puppeteer, magician's assistant, seller of tax shelter annuities (whatever they were. A family friend had set her up with that short-lived job) – she would eventually, miraculously arrive at her destination, all in a cheery, happy-go-lucky manner.

Cinderella, indeed! Honora shook her head as she tented the napkins on the plates, and then polished the glasses and silver at her tables. Not that there was anything wrong with Cinderella. After all, Honora had been Girl #6 (a brief appearance, no lines) in a high school play about Cinderella. And she and her sisters had loved the yearly TV reruns of the Rodgers and Hammerstein musical starring the very pretty and sooty Leslie Ann Warren.

Any tale of transformation served as a welcome thread to strengthen and shape the fabric of life. Only Honora's fabric of life was always knotty and uneven, with gaps and broken threads. Yet every now and then, a beautiful patch would emerge, and she would stop in awe to admire the wondrous cloth of her creation.

But Cinderella? Honora shook her head. She was Mr. Magoo. Through and through.

Throughout the pre-theater rush, and the more leisurely late diners, and then the after-theater dessert crowd, Honora thought about the little girl searching for her fallen star. Honora jotted notes down on the back of her pad where the specials were written down (she was supposed to memorize them, but sometimes she needed a quick glance – did the roast duck come with pears or apricots? Or was it raisins tonight?) The story slowly took shape. Would the little girl have a pet? A best friend? No. She would go it alone.

Such a child would search for her falling star – and find it. Honora was a firm believer in happy endings. Perhaps the little girl in the story was like her, she thought. Or like a little daughter she might one day have. In the fairytale, there would be magic. Kindness. Beauty. Wonderment. And the search for a falling star. That was as solid a start as any.

Two days later she had her draft, and two weeks after that, she had finished the story and was ready for the next assignment.

The Fallen Star

When Sophie went to bed at night, she always parted the curtains and gazed upon the night sky. Some nights, she saw patterns in the stars. Some nights, wisps of clouds sailed past a soft full moon. Some nights, she even saw a moonbow.

When the sky was especially starry, she would remember her grandmother saying, "Everybody has a star."

Sophie wondered which one was hers. There was one star that she noticed the most. It seemed to be winking at her. She tried an experiment to discover if the star was really hers. She winked and blinked with one eye and with two – and sure enough, each time the star winked back. Sophie was very happy to have found her star.

Night after night, the last thing she did before sleeping was wink at her star. One night, she was almost asleep, looking at her star between long sleepy blinks, when all of a sudden – Swhissshh! The star streamed through the sky and was gone!

Sophie kneeled up in bed with her hands on the window ledge and searched the sky. But there was no sign of her star. It had fallen.

"I must find my star," she said.

The next morning, she packed a bag with all the items she would need for her search. First of all, cookies and a sandwich. Next, a compass, though she wasn't sure how it worked. And since she didn't have a map, she brought along a tiny toy globe with bright blue oceans. Last of all, she packed a small box to put her star in – because she was sure she would find it.

Sophie set out on her journey, looking far and wide and up close. Her plan was simple: to search for something shiny. She walked and walked, and rambled and ambled. Every now and then, she climbed a fence or a tree or a hill, and shielding her eyes with her hands, she peered as far as she could see. If she spotted a flicker or a sparkle or a twinkle or a glitter, she would set off in that direction.

In the middle of the day, Sophie sat down by a tree and ate her sandwich. She took out the small globe and turned it round and round, wondering where on earth her star could be. She held the compass in her palm, but it didn't tell her anything. She thought of all the things she had mistaken for her star: a shiny beetle, sparkling dew drops, weathervanes and mailboxes, windows reflecting in the sun, and a glittering stream. She gave a deep sigh. There were many shiny things in the world.

Sophie followed the glittering stream that ran along a narrow road. At the end of the road, she saw a cottage with a blue arched door and a garden. A big garden. It was being tended by a little old man wearing a bright red vest, a blue shirt, and green pants, and a little old lady wearing a bright red skirt, a green blouse, and a blue shawl. They both wore yellow boots.

They smiled at her with twinkling eyes. A sign, perhaps? Sophie wondered.

They had just watered their garden and silvery drops clung to every leaf and petal and stem and glittered in the afternoon sun. It was a very sparkly place. Could her star be here? She was sure this place held a clue.

The old couple sensed that Sophie was searching for something.

"Can we help you find anything?" they asked.

"I'm – I'm looking for something shiny."

"Like a mirror?" asked the old man.

"Like a lake?" said the old woman.

"No," said Sophie, giving it some thought. "Something small and shiny."

"Ah! Like a coin?" suggested the old woman.

"Or like a puddle?" asked the old man.

"Like a goldfish? Like an apple? Like a ring?" they asked.

Sophie slowly shook her head to all these shiny things.

Then the old man and woman smiled at each other and said at the same time, "Like a star?"

"Yes!" cried Sophie. "Just like a star! My star! It fell from the sky last night and I can't find it anywhere. Have you seen it?"

"No," said the old man. "We haven't seen any stars around here. But we know about lost things."

"Oh, yes," the old woman agreed, chuckling. "We have lost many things in our long lives."

Sophie grew hopeful. "Can you help me find my star? Will you tell me what you know?"

"Of course," they said. "To begin with, some things aren't meant to be found."

"And some things don't want to be found."

This wasn't very helpful. "What else?" asked Sophie.

"Some things go where you can't follow."

"But nothing ever truly goes away."

This was worse. This was nonsense. They were confusing her with all their advice. Sophie felt farther from her star than ever. She thanked them politely and turned back to the road.

"There's one more thing," cried the old man.

"Never give up!" they said together.

"Never," said the old woman.

"Ever," said the old man.

"That would be silly," said the old woman.

"That would be useless," said the old man.

"Then you would never find anything."

"At all." They chuckled again, at the mere idea.

It did make sense. But all this walking and searching, and all those words made Sophie weary. She waved goodbye to them. With merry, sparkling eyes, they waved back.

Sophie meandered further along the stream. Their words tumbled around her mind as she pressed on. Some things aren't meant to be found . . . Some things don't want to be found . . .

"I'm tired."

She came across a mossy spot on the bank that looked so soft and green and inviting that she lay down on it to rest. Her eyes were just beginning to close, when to her surprise she saw something twinkling and winking just in front of her. It seemed that right before her was her star!

Sophie reached forward and picked up a little glittering rock. It sparkled just like her star. She tried her experiment, winking and blinking with one eye and with two. And sure enough, each time it blinked and winked back at her. She took out the little box from her bag, rested the rock safely inside, and tucked it into her bag.

She skipped and ran and twirled all the way back. When she passed the little cottage she waved and cried, "I found it!"

The old couple, bent over their garden, laughed and waved.

By the time Sophie arrived home, it was getting dark. Though she was tired from her adventure, she had a bowl of hot soup, and took a nice warm bath.

Before she climbed into bed, she took her star-rock from the little box and set it on her window ledge.

When the light was turned off, she parted the curtains and gazed upon the night sky. It was especially starry that night. And in the dark, the little rock glittered just like the stars and even looked like it was up in the sky with them.

Sophie winked goodnight to her rock and to the stars and very soon she fell asleep.

The End

❧

The triumph of Sophie encouraged Honora. It gave her a sense of hope. Like Sophie – indeed, like Mr. Magoo – she, too, would ultimately find what she was looking for. All she had to do was keep trying.

She had Nora to thank for pushing the story through to completion. Though Honora was forever trying to keep bossy Nora in check – being far more comfortable with Honey – Nora had a strong will and once she got an idea in her head, there was no stopping her.

In an unintentional response to that silly cartoon question, Honora envisioned Nora as a sort of Wonder Woman, Superwoman – bold, fearless, standing with legs apart, hands on hips, chin tipped up in readiness for action. Her captivating outfit in strident red and bold blue was finished off with a whip in hand. Not that she would ever use it. There was nothing of violence in Nora at all. But she liked the loud snap, the dramatic flick of her wrist. Everything about her said: *Don't mess with me. I'll take care of that. There's no challenge too great for me, go ahead and try me!*

(Honey, curled up in a long floral skirt in rose-petal pink and soft green, gave an amused chuckle at Nora. *"She's all bluster."*)

"But she does get things done," Honora answered, in Nora's defense.

(Honey sighed and languidly turned the page of the novel she was reading.)

Honora was used to their sparring. The Honey and Nora team had always been there, for as long as she could remember. She recalled a bright childhood morning, at play in her favorite (Honey-like) dress, pale blue sprinkled with white flowers. She played with her favorite (Nora-like) toy, a green John Deere tractor that she rode round and round the driveway, sometimes recklessly taking the turns on two wheels.

Honora reread "The Fallen Star." She would send this piece to one of the many publishing houses in New York City, and perhaps to a few agents. There was still a chance for everything to turn out right, wasn't there? She added a line at the top of the next page.

"We are all full of future." – HG. And she went to bed.

Honora purchased her first desktop computer, which took up her entire desk. She paid $300 for an introductory class, most of which was spent on controlling the mouse cursor, which kept running off the screen. (Mouse? She wished it had been called something else. The pointer, the sparrow, the plastic blob.) At any rate, she would have to master the computer and the mouse if she was going to make this writing thing work.

Is April a time or a place? Honora wondered. Right now, as she looked out her window, the rain gurgling in the gutters, the trees full of white blossoms and tiny bright leaves against a pearl-gray sky, it seemed a place – a land of beginnings, of youth, of beauty, a place to breathe deeply and stroll through, to enjoy its flowers and first greens, the cool soft air. She grabbed an umbrella and decided to wander through Central Park, down the Poet's Walk to the lake, and absorb the April beauty.

In the lull between the dinner and after-theater crowd, Honora worried about having enough money to pay the rent, take more classes, and buy a pair of warm winter boots. She sighed. Money!

(*"What we need is a career,"* said Nora. *"No,"* countered Honey, cringing at the word, *"what we need is an uplifting path of beauty to pursue."*)

What an enigma money was. Honora just didn't get it. It wasn't for lack of trying. She had contemplated many ways of making money.

Perhaps her favorite was the trapeze artist, an idea that was born after seeing a performer at a small circus in San Francisco, where Honora had lived for a few years. A beautiful young woman in a spangled red costume, so at ease as she sat high above the crowd, swinging, leaning back and then forward to gain momentum. Sunlight hit the moving spangles, as if she were a bird in flight. Then she dropped, suspended from the bar, and after gaining speed, (gasp!) she gracefully released, flipped, and caught the hands of another. Magic! Honora had clung to that career choice with great affection for many years.

Even now, while the waiters prepared their stations, singing the latest Broadway show tunes, Honora sometimes hummed, "she flies through the air with the greatest of ease, the daring young girl, on the flying trapeze." She kept the idea of the wondrous career tucked inside her imaginary "Favorite Dreams Box" – full of things that had never happened and yet had become a part of who she was.

Honora re-examined the other job ideas she had entertained over the years. Artist, actress, travel photographer, archeologist, astronomer, entrepren – she couldn't even finish the word, so vague, so foreign, was the idea. It fell under the odd-man-out-category of "Business," but it had a nice ring to it . . . a word with an open ending, limitless possibilities. (*But wouldn't that require math and spreadsheets?* asked Honey, quashing that idea.)

One by one, these dream careers floated away like helium balloons of different colors, mere rainbow dots up in the aquamarine sky. She gave up the careers in science (after majoring in literature), relinquished the idea of trapeze artist (no upper body strength), and though the path of acting held enormous appeal (especially to Honey, who loved costumes), Honora was too shy to face an audience with stage lights on her.

What remained was writing. It retained the sense of exploration and discovery as with archeology and travel photography, and the sense of wonder of astronomy. It held the drama of the theater, and the wistfulness of the trapeze artist. Besides, it was what she did all the time anyway.

She (and Honey) doubted her business ability, for even a writing career encompassed the entrepre – thing. And Nora remained skeptical as to the viability of such an artsy career. (*"Artsy!"* Honey hated that belittling word. But Nora demanded, *"What if such a 'career' fails to produce an income? It's not practical!"*)

To keep the peace, Honora agreed with both. To Honey, she conceded that they would refer to her writing endeavor as a "path" rather than a "career." To Nora, she conceded that such a "path" would have to be supplemented with – with – something. A bridge to be crossed at a later point. (Nora folded her arms and slowly shook her head.)

Honora spent days, weeks, months in cafés, on park benches, at her kitchen table – seeing, describing, listening. Adding bits of New York City, story ideas, and impressions to the pages of her notebook. Training her eye to see, her heart to feel, her mind to capture, and relying on Honey and Nora to weave it all together. The notebook cover became creased from being opened so many times, and the corners softened with wear. It grew into a mini world of its own.

"Café on Cornelia Street." Late afternoon, autumn. I sit alone at the table here and think: this is the thing about NYC. At the table across from me, there are two deaf gay guys, talking with their hands. You must come to a city like this, the more things you have that set you apart. The third-world people hoping for better lives, the artists, the wild ones, the lonelies, the eccentrics, the dreamers – all are welcome here, are part of here.

A group of schoolchildren just walked-ran-stumbled past the window – eating brown bread? The woman with them has bright purple hair – and she is carrying a fishing pole. None of that makes any sense at all.

At the table to my right, sit a black man and a white man. The black man is wearing white, the white man is wearing black. They are discussing some new discovery in space. A black-hole galaxy, something like that. One is explaining to the other, using his hands to describe lightyears and bent light and gravitational forces.

In the corner is a table of three women – 40s, 50s, 60s. Scarves, beads, flamboyant jackets, fly-away gray hair. I see they are free. One speaks with an Irish accent, and I catch words like "Belfast," and "I was the one in the hunger strike." They are happy, with many sudden bursts of laughter. I like these people who have, not just a cheerfulness about them or an underlying optimism, but a sense that they are making an occasion out of life.

A couple comes in and the woman is wearing a beautiful coat that I recently saw in a favorite boutique of mine. It cost $800, so I just admired it, stroked its velvet collar and admired the lovely blue-green color. How did she get the money? I wonder.

I really don't understand the money thing. Maybe she charged it.

Now the sun is setting on Cornelia Street. Setting earlier because we just switched from Daylight Savings Time. I never got that either.

And now two policemen pass by the window. They seem kind. The waiter sets a lit candle on my table; evening is overtaking the day. Time to go.

Honora walked to the music store between shifts on a crisp November day. It was one of her escape havens from the restaurant, just a few blocks away. An interesting atmosphere, an assortment of people playing pianos: a slender Asian woman with delicate hands; a large, bearded man who demonstrated the timbre of different keyboards to a customer; an older gentleman seated, playing as if he was in his own home; and the very tentative Honora.

Standing, she played a few chords, a few notes from Fauré's "Pavane." Hearing the other people play with confidence created a yearning, a wish that she had devoted more time to studying music. A wish that she had a room with a piano. It had been so long since she had a piano of her own to play, before she had moved away from her hometown. Filled with the melody of someone playing Bach's "Fugue in G minor" and the haunting longing to be more than she was, she left the music store and wandered a few blocks down.

She regretted that she never could play without sheet music, and never did learn theory. She realized that almost everything she did, and everywhere she went, she was never on *terra firma*. There was no area of expertise, no realm of knowledge that granted her confidence and authority. Even with her degree in literature, she felt at odds with the academics, so firm in their opinions and jargon. She remained skeptical of all their theories and pontificating and wished they would just talk about the stories themselves. She once listed, off the top of her head, all the theorists that came to mind – and gave up when she got to around thirty, realizing that only two of them were women.

Walking through the Times Square neighborhood, Honora was struck afresh by the city. Though living and working only blocks away, she usually avoided the touristy crowds of Times Square. But today, she saw it through fresh eyes – the insistent vitality of the neighborhood. Narrow side streets, carts and street vendors everywhere, traffic and pedestrians all over the place vying for progress in their destinations. It was thrilling, jarring, and aggressive – yet attractive in its way. Harsh, brash, gray, gritty – and vibrantly alive.

The neighborhood, the music store, the writing she had done at her table in the morning, all came together and reminded her of when she first came to the city. So full of dreams and excitement. So open, so hungry for experience and knowledge. Her earlier, artistic self re-awoke, and she found herself once more delighted to be here in the thick of struggle, here in the high drama that was New York City.

This will be enough, she thought. Just to be a part of it. Safely on its periphery, but close enough to be dazzled by its energy and tension and raw beauty. She would take that energy and beauty and process it, shape it into something.

Describe, describe. I exited the subway stairs on a damp and cold Monday morning, the bare trees of the park just ahead of me. A young woman, dressed in a black knee-length coat, black tights, and little black boots walked briskly ahead of me (there was something of the Nora swagger about her).

She lightly tossed her mass of dark coppery curls that hung to the middle of her back, the kind of hair that in sunlight would have crackled with a thousand glints of gold, now a dull burnished copper in the gray of morning. She strode with her feet slightly splayed. Between the hem of her black coat and her boots, a set of pugnacious calves. Whatever was on her list of things to do that day, she was sure to get them done.

Central Park – Honora's backyard. She played tourist when friends and family visited, seeing it all through fresh eyes once more. The Belvedere Castle, the Shakespeare Garden, the Swedish Marionette Cottage.

Honora reminisced how it was a job as a puppeteer that had got her to New York City in the first place. She had been visiting her friend in upstate New York, wondering how she could make the move from the West Coast (by then, she was living in Seattle) to the East Coast. They had gone to a puppet show where an acquaintance of her friend was performing. She explained that the troupe toured the local schools and libraries and put on shows at various events. The puppets were large, hand-crafted figures on long sticks that the puppeteers used to animate them. Wizards and princesses, ogres and fairies. Enchanting, magical!

The friend had told Honora that one member would be going on maternity leave and they would need a replacement. Since Honora had dabbled in acting and taken a few classes, they offered her the job. Honora was sold. She would become a puppeteer!

She had said goodbye to Seattle, driven across country in a car packed with her belongings, and brushed up on the history of puppets. Only to discover upon arriving that the troupe had disbanded. (Nora pointed out: *That was never a very solid career choice.* Honey sighed. *But you have to admit, those puppets were magnificent.*)

Honora treated herself to an afternoon at the beautiful Pierpont Morgan Library, a space both grand and intimate, opulent and reverent. Painted vaulted ceilings, luxurious details in wood and stone and fabric, rich colors – a jewel of a museum full of exquisite treasures and a magnificent collection of illuminated manuscripts and rare books. Centuries upon centuries of treasures of the mind and spirit, the quest that seeks out the best of what we could be. Humbling, and inspiring. Her own studies had been a mere dip into the vast world of knowledge and beauty.

Some people are so beautiful, Honora thought. There was a different kind of beauty in this city. More varied, more exotic. Like the young girl at the grocery checkout, who looked exactly like Nefertiti. Dark skinned and luminous, casually ringing up and bagging groceries, seemingly unaware of how stunning she was. Like that Japanese woman who sat demurely at a four-top last night. Exquisite. Long black hair to her waist, a striking face that caused everyone to stare at her.

And like that man who came in two days ago for a business lunch meeting. Golden skinned, strong features, a deep voice. Handsome in all the ways she thought of as masculine. He was beautiful in a deeply stirring way. When his eyes caught Honora observing him, she turned away, blushing and suddenly self-conscious.

She was thrilled when he returned for a few more meetings. And then, once, alone.

❧

It began with tentative conversations. Strolls through Central Park and – (*"Wrong notebook!"* chided Nora.)

❧

The sunset sky was achingly beautiful. Soft, mysterious. Shades of lavender, gold, and unexpected robust pink. A sky both tender and passionate.

❧

Over the weekend, Honora meandered throughout the Upper West Side in a happy frame of mind. They wound their way through the flea market where he purchased her an Egyptian vial of amber-scented oil in thin gold glass, and she bought him a wooden incense burner inlaid with brass. They strolled down Columbus Avenue, stopping for refreshment, and cut through the plaza of Lincoln Center. She paused to admire a poster of a ballerina arched effortlessly in beauty. They circled the plaza and rested on the rim of the fountain, watching the water shoot up in rhythmic splendor, while Honora kept snatching glimpses of his beautiful face.

Late at night, she sat at her desk, jotting down her recollections and softly smiling. ("*Wrong notebook*," reminded Nora, once again.) "But it's all connected," argued Honora. She picked up her rarely-used diary and indulged her feelings.

Honora now sat at her kitchen table and tried to work on the next assignment for her children's writing class, but her mind kept wandering. She remembered the recent stroll and the ballet poster, and thought perhaps she would write about a ballerina. In the margins of her notebook, she sketched a tutu. Then a ballerina in a floating gown.

But another image kept reappearing, and she gave into it. She saw a beautiful home with a cozy study where she could read books, learn about history and literature, science and the arts. It would have a large globe, maybe an old astrolabe on one of the shelves, and a fireplace. Always a fireplace. And in the winter, she would make a cup of tea and sit in the armchair . . .

Maybe she could combine the ideas of books, lamps, and cups of tea, with the beauty of the ballet. Though Honora intended to write a tale of candlelit learning and dance, it soon wound its way into a love story about a scholar. A scholar ant, to be specific, who lived in a tree trunk. And a ballerina who lived near him – in a shoebox. Honora let the idea bump around in her mind as she got ready for work.

After a long and busy night at the restaurant, Honora trudged home in a drenching rain that her umbrella did nothing against. She arrived home soaked, cold, and uninspired – not in the mood to work on her fairytale.

(*"Don't wait for the muse to appear!"* Nora bullied. Honey rolled her eyes. *"You read that in a book somewhere."*

Nora was very good at some things: following directions, getting things done on time, even editing, but originality wasn't one of them. *"Sorry, Nora, but you know it's true."*

A snap of the whip!

Honey blew out a soft puff of air. *"Besides, I happen to be on good terms with our muse. I know how to bring her forth."*

A snort from Nora prompted Honey to prepare a hot bath with amber-scented water. Afterwards, a cup of tea.)

Warm and somewhat inspired now, Honora sipped on the tea and gazed at the sky outside her window, the apartment buildings with fire escapes, the trees, all softly illuminated by diffused city light. Honora opened the notebook and pondered the fairytale. Below the tutu and gown she drew a tree trunk.

(*"That doesn't count! That's a drawing,"* said Nora, annoyed that Honey's tricks always worked. Honey simply turned her shoulder against Nora, curious to see more.)

Honora continued to draw as the story took place in her mind. A large tree trunk, with a tiny arched door. Tiny arched windows going up the trunk. Far up, before the branches began, a little balcony, with a table and umbrella. Inside, walls lined with books, books, books. And more books. A scholar's home. Thaddeus the Scholar Ant's home. Cozy fireplace, snug kitchen, lamplight over his winged-back reading chair, tobacco-y vanilla-scented smoke curling up from his pipe . . .

Thaddeus & Emma

Deep in the Faraway Forest alongside the Rippling River, nestled the tiny village of Berryfield. A winding road ran through the village and out to the famous berry fields – strawberries, blueberries, blackberries, boysenberries, gooseberries, and raspberries. Travelers came from near and far to visit the pretty village, and to gather its delightful berries and taste its delicious berry pies, berry muffins, and berry jams.

Not far from the berry fields stood a large old oak tree where Thaddeus the ant lived. A bit further downstream, tucked away among the berry brambles and forest ferns, was a shoebox, the home of Emma, the beautiful ballerina, who was also well-known for her raspberry preserves and blueberry muffins (though her pies never turned out quite right).

Attached to the shoebox was a flower-filled platform garden with benches, a table and chairs. Inside her home sat a pink music box with a small stage. When the lid was opened, tiny tinny music poured forth, and Emma positioned herself on the stage and twirled and twirled.

Since she danced all the time, she always dressed in her long, flowing ballet skirts, a different color for each day of the week. On Sunday she wore her satiny white skirt, on Monday her pale-blue skirt with sparkles, on Tuesday her emerald-green skirt scalloped in gold, on Wednesday her lavender skirt overlaid with white lace, on Thursday a simple black skirt covered in pink rosettes, on Friday a peacock blue skirt that shimmered between all the shades of blue and green (her favorite), and on Saturday her multicolored plaid skirt (Thaddeus's favorite).

Thaddeus was Emma's best friend. He was a scholar ant who lived just outside the village in a hollowed-out tree trunk. High up on the tree Thaddeus built a deck where he took many of his meals, if the weather was fine. Sometimes he even set up a cot out there and slept under the treetops, listening to the night sounds of the forest and the Rippling River.

Inside, his home was filled with rows of bookshelves, completely lining the trunk, with spiral staircases and ladders connecting them all. He loved to read and study, and his curiosity and capacity to learn had no bounds.

On winter evenings, he liked to build a cozy fire in the fireplace, rest his feet on the green velvet ottoman, and smoke his pipe while he read. Sometimes his friend Old Ned, an aged grasshopper, stopped by to discuss ideas or borrow a book, especially on nights when the grasshopper's wife, Old Peg, was at her quilting bee.

Thaddeus often took his walking stick and ambled over to Emma's shoebox. In fair weather, they strolled through the forest, and with his magnifying glass and sketchbook, Thaddeus catalogued the local plants and flowers, while Emma spread a picnic lunch and gathered flowers and berries. Then they returned home and sat at the table in Emma's flower garden and enjoyed a cup of tea and berry muffins on Emma's blue dotted china.

In cold or stormy weather, Emma visited Thaddeus at his home, and together they studied maps, or worked jigsaw puzzles, or simply chatted in front of a dancing fire, sipping on hot cocoa.

And sometimes, in all kinds of weather, they met their friends at the Forest Café and enjoyed a sunny lunch or a lamp-lit dinner, where they often prevailed upon Old Ned to perform a little soft-shoe, while Old Peg played the piano and sang.

All in all, they were very happy.

Except for one thing. Emma deeply loved Thaddeus, but she was never quite sure if he loved her. She imagined that Thaddeus thought she was not learned enough for him, for she was just a dancer.

And Thaddeus was deeply in love with Emma, but he was afraid to tell her because she was a beautiful ballerina full of vitality and excitement, and he was just a stuffy old scholar. To Thaddeus, Emma was better than any princess he had ever read about in any book. It would be a dream come true, a fairytale come true, if Emma would one day join her life with his.

Thaddeus's knowledge was wide and deep, and he had read all his books at least twice, but the thing he was most famous for in the village was his kindness. He helped the schoolchildren with their letters and numbers and geography.

He delivered firewood and tasty berry treats to his elderly neighbors. He helped several people to build or repair their homes. And he helped Emma with her gardening and baking and shopping and anything else he could possibly think of. To Emma, and to the folk who knew him, Thaddeus was a true prince.

Which was a funny coincidence. Because even though Thaddeus was just an ant, rumors persisted on the forest floor that in reality he *was* a prince – the frog-like kind who becomes a prince when kissed by his truly beloved. The old-timers who remembered the olden days believed in the tale, but everyone else thought it was nonsense – especially the frogs, who thought he was trying to cut in on their fairytales.

Thaddeus didn't pay attention to the rumors. He was happy with his books and his friends and neighbors – though his burning love for Emma caused him daily anguish. Sometimes he would stop in the middle of climbing a spiral staircase to retrieve a book and fall into a daze, dreaming of Emma, and forget why he was on the stairs.

Or he would get to the end of reading a book and realize that he didn't know what he had read – it was as if the whole book had said Emma Emma Emma Emma Emma Emma Emma Emma Emma Emma. Then he would close the book, fetch his walking stick, and go on a long ramble through the forest, deep in thought, thinking that the only thing to make him feel like a prince would be if the lovely and talented Emma would marry him. But, as he knew, such things only happened in fairytales.

One day, the hundred-year storm arrived, taking everyone by surprise, except the old-timers who remembered the olden days and knew it was coming. They tried to warn everyone, but no one would listen.

Thaddeus knew it was coming because he had read about it in several of his books. He prepared for it by adding strong shutters to his tree trunk windows, stocking up on firewood, and caulking the front door. Thaddeus helped Emma to secure her shoebox by tying strong ropes over the top and anchoring them to tree roots.

On the day of the storm, Thaddeus and Old Ned and Old Peg passed Emma as they headed to the Forest Café. They invited her to join them, but she was on her way to gather berries from the forest. She told them she would bake a boysenberry pie that they could all enjoy out on Thaddeus's deck. Thaddeus studied the clouds and told Emma to stay close to the village, as the hundred-year storm might well arrive that very day.

In Emma's kitchen hung a shelf with different colored pails for each kind of berry: a blue pail for blueberries, a bright red one for strawberries and a soft red one for raspberries, a purple pail for boysenberries, a purplish-black one for blackberries, and a light-green pail for gooseberries. Today, Emma carried the green pail and the purple pail, which both went nicely with her multicolored plaid skirt, she couldn't help but notice.

She walked to the berry fields and all along the forest paths where the best gooseberries and boysenberries grew, pirouetting now and then, or stopping for an occasional plié with her pails held out beside her. She hummed and sang and thought of the delicious pies she would make when she got home. Maybe the crust would turn out right this time and Thaddeus would be pleased.

But while she was on her way back home, she noticed that the sky was getting darker and darker. She decided to take the shorter river path back to her shoebox.

Just as Thaddeus and Old Ned and Old Peg finished their lunch, the wind began to blow, and the sky became a turbulent gray. Large drops of rain began to fall, and then a pelting rain hammered the café tables. The café owners gathered the teacups and saucers that were blowing around the café garden and hung a sign on the door saying *Back After Storm.*

Since Thaddeus's home was closer, he convinced Old Ned and Old Peg to stay with him until the storm passed. They made their way to Thaddeus's tree trunk with their heads bent against the wind and rain. Thaddeus told them to go on ahead and make themselves comfortable, while he made sure that Emma was snug in her shoebox.

Thaddeus imagined them all later sitting around his fire, eating pie and drinking tea, after the storm had passed. As he neared Emma's house, he could almost smell the boysenberry pie that should be cooling just about now. But when he knocked on her door, he was alarmed to find that she was not at home.

By now the wind was blowing in heavy gusts, tossing leaves and pinecones and birds' nests in the air (some of them with birds still in them, chirping and flapping their wings).

Thaddeus was glad he had brought his sturdy umbrella, for it was raining forcefully now, a true giant of a storm. With heavy, thunderous boots, the storm clomped and stomped and bellowed and brawled through the forest, thrashing the trees and snapping thick branches as if they were sticks, flailing wild arms to grab at the sky and wring hard rain from the clouds, blowing angry gusts at the river and creating whitecaps in the churning water. Stomp! Stomp! Stomp! The storm marched through the forest, howling, crashing, kicking at rocks and roots and whatever was in its path.

The forest folk were tucked away safely inside their homes, shutters pulled, doors bolted, and a few with the bedcovers pulled over their heads. All except for Thaddeus, who could barely hold on to the forest fence rail as he searched for Emma. He called out again and again but didn't hear an answer. Then he began to run along the forest path to the river which was already swollen with rain.

He stopped when he heard a tiny voice in between the wail of the wind – "Help! Help!"

Thaddeus ran to the river's edge, and saw Emma coming down the river, balancing herself on an upside-down café table that had blown from the Forest Café. Emma was using the table legs to navigate the angry current, steering the table away from broken tree branches. Miraculously, she was still holding the pails of berries on each arm.

"Hold on Emma! I'll save you!"

Thaddeus's reading came in handy, and he acted quickly. He pulled down a vine from a nearby tree and tied it securely around the trunk. Then he made a quick loop on the other end and, lasso-like, he hurled it across the river catching it around a tree stump on his first try. He tightened it just as Emma's table passed under the rope and she quickly grabbed the vine. Thaddeus turned his umbrella upside down, stepped inside, and pulled himself along the vine until he reached Emma.

"Climb aboard, Emma!"

Emma stepped into the umbrella, and together they fought the rushing current, pulling along the vine with all their strength. The vine held just until they stepped onto the shore, when it snapped and shredded into pieces and went sailing down the river.

Thaddeus shook out the umbrella and held it over them, pointing it into the storm, and carried the pails of berries in his other hand. When they came to her shoebox, they found that it was surrounded with water, so they trudged on to Thaddeus's tree trunk.

Old Ned and Old Peg were watching from the window and rushed to open the door to welcome them home.

Emma breathlessly recounted the watery rescue as they climbed the three stone stairs and stepped inside the dry trunk.

"Whoa!" cried Old Ned, on hearing of his friend's bravery. "Astounding!" Old Ned had to grab hold of the door to steady himself against the wind. "The most amazing river rescue I've ever heard of – for Thaddeus doesn't know how to swim!"

"Oh, Thaddeus!" cried Emma. "You risked your life to save me!"

Just as they were closing the door, a tree limb flew through the air and hit Thaddeus on the head, knocking him to the ground. Old Ned pulled Thaddeus inside and put all his weight on the door to close it, and Old Peg quickly bolted it.

Emma knelt down beside Thaddeus and tears filled her eyes on seeing his motionless form. Then he slowly blinked open his eyes and smiled to see Emma leaning over him.

"How's your head, Thad?" asked Old Ned.

"Fine, fine. Nothing a cup of tea won't fix."

Emma had her arm under Thaddeus's neck. On hearing him sound like his old self, she leaned forward and said, "Oh, Thaddeus!" And she kissed him.

Then three loud gasps came from Emma, Old Ned, and Old Peg. Their hands flew to their mouths, and they stood back in awe. For on Thaddeus's head, there appeared a crown.

"Aha! I always knew it!" said Old Ned.

"So it *is* true!" cried Old Peg.

"My prince!" said Emma.

Thaddeus put a hand to his head and smiled. "Emma, my princess, will you marry me?"

"Of course! I've been waiting for you to ask."

Thaddeus smiled. "Then my fairytale dream will come true."

So, Thaddeus and Emma were married and lived happily ever after. Thaddeus was still an ant, but a prince ant. Being modest, however, he never wore the crown and set it on one of the bookshelves along with rocks and pinecones and vases of flowers that Emma picked.

They decided to move Emma's shoebox and platform garden next to Thaddeus's tree trunk so that Emma could still practice her ballet and bake muffins and pies and enjoy them out among her flowers. But a question arose.

"However will I get my shoebox to your tree?"

Thaddeus gave a small chuckle. "Emma, Emma, Emma. You forget what I am."

She clasped her hands to her cheek. "A prince?"

"No, an ant."

He issued a whistle that only ants could hear. Throughout the forest floor, one by one, all ants dropped what they were doing and assembled near the shoebox.

"Hello, Thad. You called?"

With Emma and Thaddeus seated on top of the shoebox, the ants lifted the box and followed his directions. It moved along the forest floor as if floating by magic, a smooth and scenic ride. Thaddeus and Emma waved at the forest creatures who lined up to watch the spectacle.

Just as effortlessly, the ants lowered the box next to the tree trunk and then went back to building and carpentering and carrying.

"I have to say, it looks rather well here," said Emma.

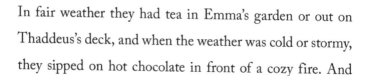

In fair weather they had tea in Emma's garden or out on Thaddeus's deck, and when the weather was cold or stormy, they sipped on hot chocolate in front of a cozy fire. And sometimes, in all kinds of weather, they met their friends at the Forest Café and enjoyed a sunny lunch or a lamp-lit dinner and prevailed upon Old Ned to perform a little soft shoe, while Old Peg played the piano and sang.

And when the village children, who had heard the recent rumors, asked Thaddeus if he was or wasn't a prince, he just smiled and winked at Emma. "That depends if you believe in fairytales."

The End

Nothing compares to love, thought Honora. (Even Nora smiled at the ending.)

The choices of classes and bookstores and readings were a writer's paradise. Libraries everywhere, the Main Library a gold mine and breathtakingly beautiful. Honora was almost overwhelmed by the variety and opportunities in this most writerly of cities.

"Earthly Paradise." One of Honora's favorite haunts was The Strand – "18 miles of books." A haven. A land just waiting to be explored. Adventures abounded in those shelves. After periodically accumulating too many hardcovers and paperbacks, Honora would gather a bag of read books, lug them onto the subway, and carry them down to 12th Street. Then she would haul them to the front counter to sell back – gape at the pittance offered – accept the offer and buy some more.

One day, on a whim, she asked the man at the front counter if they had any books by Kathleen Norris. Honora's grandmother had been a writer of sorts who had corresponded with the prolific author in the 1920s.

Honora was directed through the labyrinth to a shelf where she found several copies of old hardcover books. She inhaled the scent of years between the faded covers and chose two. Perhaps she would slowly put together a small collection. She noticed a newer book by Kathleen Norris and purchased it as well, assuming it was a reprint.

She took them home and began to read the newer book, only to realize that it was written by a different Kathleen Norris. One very much alive. A poet and essayist. Honora glanced at the attractive cover, *The Cloister Walk*, and flipped through the book. It was her account of the period she spent in a Benedictine monastery.

Honora stretched out on her bed, stacked pillows to prop herself up, and browsed through the book. Hmm, she thought. Kind of interesting. A whole other way to approach life. A "monastic perspective," "liturgical time," prayer, study, community. (Honey imagined candlelit spaces, medieval chanting, fragrant herb gardens, and snuggled into the read.)

Honora had to admit there was a certain appeal to all that cloistered introspection. She remembered having a similar thought when she studied *The Canterbury Tales* in one of her medieval literature classes. And learned that many wealthy women went into the convent as an alternative to marriage – a clean and safe place to practice devotion and pursue learning, with music and gardens. Not a bad option for back then.

As Honora made her way through the book, with several noncommittal "hmms" and "huhs," and a pause to look out the window, she placed her finger on a certain passage, and immediately landed in the scene described.

> *"The Cherub was stationed at the gate of the earthly paradise with his flaming sword to teach us that no one will enter the heavenly paradise who is not pierced with the sword of love." - St. Francis de Sales,* Treatise on the Love of God

Honora gave a soft smile. Oh, Cherub – so full of yourself. She frowned at the language of violence, swords, and threats. Fine, she thought, eyeing the cherub at the gate. I'll take this other earthly paradise, this earthly love.

She observed the scowling figure as he stood guard all alone – the typical cherub, chubby, puffy cheeks, stubby ornamental wings that would never lift him an inch off the ground. He was fattened on puddings and petit fours, born to privilege and the right to tell other people what to do. He looked a little glum about the mouth as he shifted from foot to foot, perhaps redistributing his weight, or perhaps in boredom. He was not happy.

Honora looked behind her at the familiar earthly paradise. She saw lush gardens, corner cafés and bookstores, lights twinkling in the balmy evening, heard the laughter of children, strains of music.

She glanced back at the cherub. She guessed that he was feeling rather superfluous at the gate – as if he hadn't chased anyone away for quite some time. She wanted to suggest a different tactic; perhaps a friendlier approach would be more effective.

She walked towards him and smiled kindly, palms up, as he raised his flaming sword in warning. She explained that she simply had a question.

He frowned in disappointment and lowered his sword.

Then she asked if he could suggest a place nearby for sweets – profiteroles, chocolates, that sort of thing.

The cherub grew animated as he recommended his favorite shops and chocolatiers and their specialties.

She thanked him and sought out the nearest one. She was soon seated on a bench in the leafy garden, its air sweet and mild, reading a book and eating chocolates from a white box embossed with lovers.

When she glanced over at the gate, she saw that the cherub was watching her, with a glimmer of longing in his eyes. She waved him over.

He looked at his flaming sword, and then at the words on the gate. He doused the sword in a bucket of water, shrugged off his wings, and opened the gate wide. Next, he laid the sword before the gate, like an arrow pointing towards the happy garden, in case anyone was looking for him.

Then the cherub joined her in the garden, sat next to her on the bench, and sampled the chocolates she offered, comparing pieces. They enjoyed the fragrant breeze, the rosebushes in bloom, and smiled at the sound of children splashing in the nearby fountain and the birdsong above them in the trees.

A seminar on getting published, picking up extra shifts at the restaurant, attending classes, poetry readings, off-off-Broadway plays, writing, writing, and filling the notebook.

Ping, ping. Honora left a trail of hairpins in her wake as she fled the restaurant. The extra shifts and today's early brunch crowd had left little time for sleep.

The previous night had been especially trying. A large private party, a winter celebration, everyone having a grand time, the women dressed beautifully, glasses clinking among laughter and conversation. Honora couldn't help but look down at her black waiter's shoes and pants, and wonder – why am I on this side of things? Why is this how I spend my Saturday nights? This is not why I came to New York City. Where did I go wrong?

Isn't there an easier way? Perhaps I'm more like Cinderella than I care to admit. An easy lift out of this existence would be welcoming. No wonder the Cinderella story had such longevity, such traction.

Honora gave up that night's dinner shift. Enough was enough. She felt far from herself and wanted to spend some time writing. It was too easy to get caught up in the bills, rent, and struggles of city life and forget why she had come here.

She shopped for groceries on her way home, her shoes offering little protection from the snow. She climbed the steps to her third-floor walkup, fixed a quick meal, and took a hot bath. Since becoming a waitress, she had developed the habit of taking a bath to wash away the day, the smells of food, the achy legs, the demands (a snap of the fingers, a wave of the hand – "Waitress! This is undercooked, too salty. I said sauce on the side! Can I have a different chair?"). The bath, a barrier between the workaday world and the night world of dreams, the world of her creation.

Honora slipped on her midnight-blue velvet skirt and thick socks, made a cup of hot chocolate, and pulled out her notebook. Outside her kitchen window, the snow was falling. Landing like whispers on the bare branches and set-tling in the forks of the trees, little white valleys. Across the back courtyard, the snow was outlining the black ironwork of the fire escapes.

Cinderella? True, she needed a change, but Honora wanted to fix her plight herself (no rescue, thank you, Prince). And yet the idea of a fairytale transformation filled her with longing. How was she going to make her dreams happen? How could she manage to stay on her beloved art-ist's path?

Like she always had. By combining Honey's love of beauty, poetry, and romance with Nora's fiery indepen-dence and determination. Honey's long skirts and beads and scarves served as glimpses into other worlds, other ways of being, windows into a romantic past – but they were at odds with Nora's more minimalist vision of practicality.

Honora drew a dollar sign in the margin, and a question mark. Her inspiration was frozen.

Perhaps it was the low spirits and fatigue, but Honora found herself sliding into Cinderella mode. She drew a turreted castle, stars around the pointed towers, a long flight of stairs.

Don't worry, Nora, she thought. *I don't see this as a way out. Rather, as a way into that world of transformation.* (Nora remained skeptical. Honey sat up in expectation.)

Honora tapped her pen on the page.

Cinderella had always been there – even when she wasn't wanted. Honora remembered how the feminists in her women's literature class had shredded the tale to pieces, the Cinderella complex and all that. (Nora had admired their confidence and capable black army boots. Allies! Honey had sat slightly embarrassed in her long flowing skirts and tucked the excess fabric under her legs, sat on her hands, and kept quiet.)

Honora had agreed with much of what her classmates said. Cinderella *wasn't* a good role model. She was too passive, for one thing (though in her defense, not as passive as Sleeping Beauty or Snow White – waiting, waiting, waiting for someone else to get things moving).

But the idea of transformation – of becoming something other than you were – that was the real crux of the tale, wasn't it? When did that Cinderella-based desire begin for her?

Honora squinted into the distant past. She remembered the schoolyard of childhood where she sang the jump rope song along with the other girls:

Cinderella dressed in blue, went upstairs to marry who?

Cinderella dressed in red, went upstairs to marry Ted (or Fred or Ned).

Cinderella dressed in pink, went upstairs to marry a fink.

. . . in white, a knight; in yellow, a fellow; green – a fiend, was it? At least there were choices.

The young Honora had considered all the colors. She certainly didn't want to marry a fiend or a fink. White, knight – not bad, but suspect. Just too good to be true.

Honora liked the question open ended and chose Cinderella dressed in blue. Cinderella, the projection of all the little girls – of what they could become when they grew older and entered the glamorous land of the teenager, or even older and could move away to some distant place where a young girl could blossom into her true self.

The story had appealed to Honora's young heart – such a beautiful, glittering spun fancy. She especially liked the pumpkin becoming a golden carriage, but still looking like a pumpkin. She could have done without the mice-footmen and just as happily driven herself to the ball. And although she loved going barefoot, there was something click-clacking wonderful about the glass slippers as Cinderella ran down the long flight of stairs.

And the prince? Oddly enough, nothing much was ever said about him. Honora suspected that he was perhaps a bit unimaginative, never having had to fend for himself. He was most likely a bit bored – and boring. In a way, he was rather peripheral to the story of transformation.

Honora gazed out at the falling snow. She drew a squiggly line in the margin to make sure the ink in her pen was flowing. What would *her* version of Cinderella look like? she wondered. (Honey and Nora both leaned forward – *"Well, let's find out,"* they said.)

"The Wanderings and Wonderings of Cinderella"

Poor Cinderella. For this Cinderella, the story was somewhat different. When she ran down the steps – that long flight of marble steps with her gossamer blue dress trailing – she let slip from her foot a glass slipper. And it fell one step to the next, down, down, down, chipping, until the very last step where it splintered into a thousand pieces.

The other shoe changed into air as the clock struck midnight. There was no way for the prince to find her now. All he had was a handful of glass shards that he couldn't make heads or tails of – for he hadn't noticed her shoes; men never do.

And all she had was the memory. Lived, felt, the dream seeping into her veins, of a richly beautiful world. For a few hours she had inhabited that world of enchantment, gliding and twirling through it, enthralled.

But now it was gone. Was it better never to have experienced it? No. She would treasure her beautiful memory and her new-found knowledge that there was wonder and splendor in the world. Entwined within the humdrum workaday world, there was magic and music and romance.

That was the secret. She would go forth into the world and search for these things, beyond the scullery work, the ashes, the mud, the mundane. Cinderella gathered her raggedy clothes about her as if they were beautiful, and fled into the woods behind the palace.

At the first mossy-banked, woodland pool she cleansed her face forever of the chimney soot. She would never go back to that chair by the chimney, that terrible place with the cruel step-mother and step-sisters.

She threw a glance in the direction of the palace. And that prince. What was so great about him? What did he ever do on his own? He had everything handed to him.

Cinderella bathed herself and washed her rags and looked at her reflection in the pool. She touched her head where the tiara had been and sighed. Her face quivered in the water's reflection.

So, she thought, *this is what I am. So. I must find out more about this thing called me. Why did I sit for so long in the corner by the chimney, smudged and crouched? Sometimes I hate myself for being so weak. Well, I am still young, able-bodied, and strong – somewhere inside. I will create my own world.*

Cinderella draped her wet rags over the flowering bushes to dry, their scent infusing the cloth (at least she imagined that it did).

She lay on the mossy bank and smiled at her new-found determination – smiled through the tears that soaked the mossy pillow beneath her head. For she had no money, no clothes, no friends, nothing at all but a dream, and a memory.

The night was mild, and the silvery starlight made her enchantingly beautiful – soft, sylvan, a fairy of the forest – in fact, the most beautiful that she would ever be! Alas, there was no one there to witness it, which was a waste, and she herself was unaware. A

peak moment, the body's moment of perfection –
gone by, unnoticed.

The next day Cinderella put on her clean rags. The
sweet scent in them lifted her spirits. *Here is a small
bit of beauty that I can always have – fresh, clean clothes
that smell of blossoms. Yes,* she thought, gathering a
few flowers and weaving them into a necklace – *why
did I never think of this? How wonderful to wear flowers. But I must get rid of these rags that are reminders
of my old ways.*

She meandered through the woods picking berries
and tasting tender shoots of greens and nibbling on
little flowers. This light repast, the fresh air, and
warm sunshine strengthened her, and she continued
on her journey.

She passed a manor house, breathtakingly lovely,
and gazed at it longingly. It was turreted, trimmed
in elegant white stone, and diamond-shaped leaded
windows opened onto gardens.

Peacocks pranced around with their magnificent
tails fanned open. One cried out and her eyes

widened at the strange, plaintive caw. *So that's what a peacock sounds like – I always wondered.* It spread its resplendent shimmery tail and strutted past small splashing fountains.

Roses bloomed around trellises and arbors, sunlight sparkled off the leaves and fountains and windows. The air around the manor seemed to glitter. She sighed at the beauty of it.

Afraid of being seen, Cinderella hugged the edge of the grounds. Behind the outbuildings in the back, she passed lines of laundry hanging out to dry. They smelled and looked so lovely – sparkling whites and billowing paisleys and florals, all waving in the gentle spring breeze. It made her smile.

She lightly touched a fluttering shawl – rosy and green and gold. It stirred something deep inside her, struck a chord of profound longing. It was the most beautiful thing she had ever seen.

All she could think of was her love for it. She unpinned it from the line, stuffed it into her blouse, and ran away from the manor house. She told herself she would borrow it for just the night.

Her heart pounded against the soft cloth as she fled. She ran into the woods and stopped at another woodland pool, drank from the cool water and splashed her heated face.

Then, shyly, sorrowfully, she took the shawl from her blouse and held it to her nose, inhaling its fresh scent, eyeing its wondrous beauty of velvet and gold threads. She buried her face in it and began to weep, then sob. She had done something low, base, poor. *I am just the opposite of this lovely piece of cloth.* And yet she loved the shawl. She studied her reflection – and saw that it was different. *So, this is how scars are formed*, she thought.

She kept the scars, and she kept the shawl. Most of the time, she kept it hidden inside her raggedy blouse. But on good days, she would sit on a warm rock or alongside a river and wrap the shawl around her and sing a silvery song, twisting the ends of the scarf in her fingers, as if it had always been hers.

After passing several villages, Cinderella came to a little, red-roofed town that she found rather charming. At least she could make a life there, support herself somehow.

She found a deserted one-room hut at the edge of the village, cleaned it and filled it with flowers and glittering stones and made a bed of moss. She spread the shawl over the moss pillow at night and it filled her head with sweetness.

She found a job in the marketplace selling bells of various sizes, an assortment of spoons, and local fruits and nuts gathered from the woods. She made just enough money for bread and potatoes and some fabric to make new clothes. At least she was no longer clad in rags.

But you can only sell so many bells, spoons, fruits, and nuts before it grows boring and wearisome. Cinderella began to feel stifled and so she found a different job at a flower stall that she enjoyed for a while. A short while.

And then she took a different job – helpmate to an older woman, wheeling her around the garden, organizing her papers. And then another job as a gardener. And then a different job, and still another one. *What's wrong with me? I seem unable to stay at one job. Perhaps I should have remained a fairytale. But I wasn't happy with that either.*

Finally, one day she closed the door of her little hut forever, saying, *Goodbye, little hut. I must go now.*

She did go on. For years, in this exhausting, itinerant manner. From one village to another, trying different jobs. Her moods often made her irritable and withdrawn. She met a lot of people along the way, but no one could quite connect with her or figure her out. How could they? How could she explain to them that briefly, she had been a part of something beautiful, and had no choice but to seek it, even a tiny taste of it, forever after. The curse and beauty of the fairytale.

Did she ever marry? Did she meet an old witch at the bottom of one those woodland pools she was so fond of who gave her a secret magic? Did she become a nanny or a cook? No, no, and no. Her dreams and hopes were beginning to grate on her nerves . . . .

Honora shut the notebook. The fairytale was starting to depress her. This version was too much like her own life, leaving the Midwest, living in San Francisco and then Seattle, moving from coast to coast, job to job. Honora had to admit that things were not working out quite as expected.

She saw that Nora had nodded off. Honey was blinking sleepily at the snowflakes floating past the window.

I must be tired. Honora changed into her nightgown, turned off the light, and climbed into bed. She stared out into the dark, thinking that perhaps those feminist students were right, and that Cinderella belonged on the shelf.

(Nora roused just long enough to help her punch up the pillow and frown in determination.)

Honora was far from admitting defeat, and there was no going back. She would figure it out tomorrow. And with that thought, and vague visions of woodland pools and laundry fluttering behind the manor, she drifted off to dreamland.

The next day was much the same as the previous days. Lunch shift, dinner shift. And then the week became much like the previous weeks. Lunch shift, dinner shift, lunch shift, dinner shift. And then the month became much like –

("*Okay! We get it!*" cried Nora. Even Honey covered her ears.)

Honora noted yet another set of new waiters and realized that she was now one of the older ones there. Some had found other jobs, some married or moved away. Even the mocking head waiter was long gone. For the first time in her life, Honora felt old. Ish. She knew she was still young, but time was racing ahead. Her poor dreams panted behind, barely keeping pace with the sprint of time. The years were passing by.

After another grueling night shift, exhausted, dispirited, Honora trudged home in the snow, reciting lines, as she often did after work, from one of her many failed poems. This one was called

"The Waitress's Lament"

So take me away, away, so far away,

For my feet are tired and my heart's been hurt.

but she never got past the wimpy refrain. (*"It sounds Cinderella-ish,"* said Nora, in a disapproving tone. *"As if you can't manage things on your own!"*)

Honora jotted down the lines at home and stared at them. *Nora's right. Mopey. Feeble.* She stuck it in the folder labeled "Bad Poetry," and pulled out another poem she had jotted down years ago on a paper napkin. Another wince-worthy wimpy poem from her years in San Francisco, entitled

"Just a Short Poem Dedicated to the First Half of My Life and What Looks Like Will Be the Second Half as Well"

Children cry,

Adults betray.

Honora gave a loud groan. "This won't do!" She shoved the napkin back into the file, groaned, and threw the whole sorry mess into the wicker waste basket. "I can't stand people who feel sorry for themselves! And that includes me!"

In the morning, she awoke with a sense of loss for her earlier self. Could she reignite the fire she had on first arriving in the city? This was supposed to be THE great beginning.

She fixed herself a cup of tea and some toast and looked at the snowy trees outside her window. She opened the notebook to the early pages to try to remember that old fire. She read a few entries and sighed at the hopefulness of her earlier self, not quite recognizing it.

Sitting at cozy Caffe Reggio, classical piano music, a gentle spring evening in the Village. Choosing plays for my scene work, and planning a life richer, fuller, the newness, the possibilities, getting closer, feeling deeper, and knowing something is going to emerge, and it's going to be wonderful.

Oh yeah, she now thought. *Caffe Reggio. I forgot about that place.* She hadn't been there for quite some time. Several years. She would go this week and pick up another notebook while she was in the Village. She was nearing the final pages of her NYC writerly Notebook Number 1.

She flipped to an early page and smiled at the section entitled, "Life in the Brownstones."

Ah yes, her first place. A room she had rented in an apartment with a bunch of strangers. Would-be actors and performers, students. Only one of them had a "real" job and she was responsible for collecting the rent. How ironic that it was *she* who had been pocketing their rent money for months, causing all of them to be evicted.

Hmm, thought Honora. She had not written about that. (*"Not in this notebook,"* said Honey. *"You have those scrappy spirals for that stuff."*) Honora read a few more entries:

The dream life will have to happen here, in this city of possibilities.

I live by the W in Wash & Dry (the vertical sign outside my window). Just off 46th Street on 9th Avenue – Part of Hell's Kitchen, in the Theatre

District, Midtown, NYC! Just around the corner from Restaurant Row. What an address!

Honora remembered how enamored she had been of that room, that neighborhood. How she had hung dried roses and hydrangeas on the white brick wall, the chinks in the brick accommodating the tiny nails. The tinted vintage pictures of old Paris that stoked the dream of living abroad one day. Lace curtains in the long windows and the old faded Victorian rug. And the $10 desk she had bought upstate when she visited her friend. She had painted it a shade of blue-green (so like a woodland pool) and it had become her writing desk. Above it she had tacked black and white postcards of famous authors: Virginia Woolf, Tennyson, HG Wells, Colette, Arthur Conan Doyle . . .

> I know it's an ugly building, the one I see outside my window. A row of tenement-like, old brick buildings. Yet sometimes, when the sunlight falls on them, the brick takes on such warmth, and the one painted rose with black trim becomes such a lovely shade. And that pale brown one takes on a softness, and I see that maybe once they were beautiful, and

that for moments now and then when the sun is shining just so, they become again, almost beautiful.

I remember that impression, Honora thought. *I remember thinking that beauty is everywhere if you just know how to find it.* She turned the page and read other entries from those early days.

> Even though my room is three floors up from Ninth Avenue, I hear everything – the voices, the sirens, the shopkeepers pulling their steel gates down at end of day, the men spitting on the street, the empty cups and bottles rolling along the sidewalk.
>
> I look around my room. Black and white posters of gardens, the floral rug, dried flowers on the walls. I call it my garden. I must have it, since I no longer see sky, or little streams turning pink in the sunset.
>
> Sometimes when the spitting and yelling become too loud outside, I turn up the volume of Satie or Chopin and the music fills the room, and I think – I live in a room of opulence. And it fills me. Like rain upon the parched earth. Like the Tinman upon

being oiled. Relief, gratefulness, the "Ahh" of welcome solace.

Honora now wondered if she had been delusional. And yet, she still believed in that happier, hopeful version of herself. Could she reclaim it?

She remembered how simple things used to flood her with joy – sitting at her kitchen table, steam curling from the black kettle. The splash of cream turning her tea a milky amber, matching the beige leaves of the cup's pink roses. Always, she could put things right, if she just had time to herself. Even after hurtful experiences, arguments, disappointments, money worries, she could always heal whole again if she could just be alone with the beautiful things, the walks, the music, the words.

Honora flipped to another page and read: "If I don't make gains every day I will surely sink." She cringed at that entry.

(Nora tapped her finger on her cheek and nodded, detective-like. *"Aha! The cracks were beginning to show even back then."*)

And another entry:

Getting off the train at Times Square, trekking through the labyrinthine passages and stairs of the subcity – the unfortunates and forgotten and beggars, the perfects whizzing by them with hard faces, the smell of urine as you instinctively step over the spit on the ground.

Among the musicians positioned here and there is a cloudy-eyed old man at a keyboard singing, *"You must remember this. A kiss is just a kiss . . ."* Such romanticism amidst the ugly is almost jarring. And yet he sings with a smile, as if believing the words. The human struggle, the words and melody weaving around it. Our collective longing for love that pervades everything.

Then, underneath the song, something strange is happening. The keyboard has a heavy strong pulse that sounds just like a heartbeat, throbbing, deep, filling the subway station, pounding the crowds, and I think – that is more appropriate, that is the real song, the primal base pulse of life, and it seems to be getting louder, louder, blending, taking over my own heartbeat. I hurry and am glad to near the turnstile to get out.

No, thought Honora. *It had not been all ease and happiness.* Getting evicted, and then finding another place that took all her salary. Again, fixing it up and falling in love with the tiny apartment, only to discover that she lived above "the crazy lady," who harassed the elderly neighbors and played pounding music late into the night. A woman who fought with everyone, including the police who were periodically called on her, and, most recently, the firemen who came to extinguish her mattress that had caught fire as she smoked in bed. She put up a fight when they explained that her pills and alcohol didn't mix and confiscated the stash of liquor she had hidden on the fire escape.

How many times after that had Honora sat up in bed and sniffed the air, wondering: Is that burnt toast? Or an apartment on fire? Or nothing at all?

It was not getting easier, that's for sure. And underlying everything was the sense of loss she felt. The ups and downs of love. Would he come back? Could he come back? Was she truly ready to commit? Nothing was clear. The fear that gripped her at living a life without him.

(Honey gave a soft, unobtrusive cough.) Honora nodded. This notebook was part of the promise to live in hope, with purpose, to further her writing career. Not for worrying. These notebooks were going to form the foundation upon which she would become her true self.

So, what's missing? The usual things, she answered. Love. Beauty. Peace. Excitement. The thrill of being on to something. Writing! Always writing. (*"So, finish some of those pieces!"* snapped Nora. Honey coaxed more gently: *"That always makes you feel better."*)

True, thought Honora. It's like the conversation with life continues, as long as I'm writing.

(Nora jumped to her feet. *"Then come on! Let's get cracking. I can feel a change a-comin'!"* Honey looked askance at Nora's odd diction.)

Honora straightened her back and nodded. *Nora's right. I must be more diligent and finish my stories. The focus has to be on the big plan, the grand dream, and not get side-tracked, as in the past.*

(Nora squared her shoulders. She had gotten credit, for once! She felt emboldened to add: *"And get a real job, Honey! It's time to grow up."* Honey was having none of it. *"Me?"* she shot back. *"You're the one who dresses like a cartoon!"*)

Honora rose to her feet, hands on her hips. It was staring her in the face. It *was* time for a change. A different job. A different apartment.

One of the waiters had told her she should try temping. She had often stared up at the office buildings and skyscrapers that filled the streets of Manhattan and wondered – what goes on in all those buildings?

It was curiosity alone that led her to entertain the idea of entering the workforce (prison bars!). Temping was the other flexible job option for the artists of the city. (Minimal commitment until that role on Broadway came through.)

The idea of change gave Honora a shot of energy, a sense of hope.

So what if she was getting older? So what if her writing submissions hadn't been accepted? She was used to making the best of things. And that was exactly what she was going to do now.

Honora smiled and parted the curtains. The night world outside was thickly covered in snow. She opened her notebook and saw that there were only a few pages left. *Might as well fill them.*

She sat at her desk and tapped the pen against the page. She would craft a plan and perhaps jot down ideas for another fairytale. Why not? She liked the happy endings.

She sketched a few images along the margins – more turrets and towers, smoke curling from high chimneys, snowflakes . . .

Beautiful eyes, golden skin, how he had kept her warm in her cold apartment. A wintery kingdom, lots of snow. A castle, of course. And love, love, love . . .

NOTEBOOK 2

ook the Second – I live in the Land of the Flying Trains! The 7 trains (lucky seven), as they round into the elevated 46th Street station in Queens, appear like flying trains as they come and go, especially at night when they're all lit up, like magical, fairytale trains. The 7 line subway station, at 46th/*Bliss* Street, in *Sunnyside*. What a happy sounding place!

Honora changed the period to an exclamation mark. First lines were always so important. She sat at her new table in her new apartment in her new neighborhood with her new notebook spread open to the first page.

She was sure she had made the right decision. Though she would have preferred a more romantic or poignant catalyst – instead of the apartment below her nearly catching on fire – she had decided to move and was happy for the change.

Goodbye to living in the Theater District, goodbye vibrant street life, goodbye Greek Orthodox Church with its incense and bells, goodbye restaurant job. Goodbye frequent strolls through her neighborhood beauty, Central Park.

Hello Queens, hello new jobs (to be determined). Hello seeing the city from a distance, another way of experiencing it. Hello and I love you Sunnyside Gardens! A tree-lined historical neighborhood of brick row houses with landscaped courtyards between them and small front gardens, window boxes filled with flowers, and potted plants on brick steps. Quaint. Built in the 1920s, a period she loved for so many reasons. (*"Not least of all the clothing,"* said Honey).

Her second-floor windows looked out on tall leafy trees and the charming row houses, some with slate roofs! There was definitely more space, more quiet – good for writing.

And when she wanted noise and excitement and museums and classes, the city was just a quick ride away. She could even see parts of the skyline from her neighborhood: the Empire State Building viewed from Queens Boulevard, the Chrysler Building as she crossed 43rd Avenue.

There was still the mini-world feel that Manhattan had, with different languages and styles of clothing and small ethnic grocery stores. Her immediate neighborhood included people from Turkey, Guyana, Ireland, Korea, Columbia, Pakistan, Germany, Mexico, Bangladesh, Austria, China, Brazil.

There were plenty of good restaurants and little cafés (where she could find work until she was more settled) and lovely neighborhood walks (though not as extensive as in Manhattan. She often crossed and recrossed the same streets in a one-hour stroll.)

Honora sighed in pleasure as she smoothed the page and looked out the window. Another beginning. Always so promising, always so wide-open happy.

And yet, she was well aware that she was now some-where in the middle of her life. If her personal drama was a three-act play, she would definitely be in Act II. Middles, as she had discovered in her writings, were always problematic. They didn't hold the punch and promise of beginnings, the tidiness and satisfaction of endings. Not to mention, middles were dominated by the troublesome plot question: Now what?

Act II already? A worrisome thought. She wanted more time. *Let's make life a five-act play.* That would keep her in Act II, perhaps edging towards Act III, but with two more acts in the far distance. *Much better.*

Honora was clearly trying to convince herself that, although the beautiful beginnings of youth were now behind her, this stage of life offered wonders of its own. However, she would have to be more judicious with her time and choices. This phase would be marked by getting closer to her dreams, with more learning, more disciplined writing, and more of her stories being submitting. (Honey added, *"And seeing more of the world. Being more, living more."* Nora remarked, *"As solid a plan as I've ever heard."*)

One year later, from the corner on Queens Boulevard, Honora stopped to watch the evening train as it rounded the curve and headed further into Queens. Lit up with golden windows, sailing into the night. She was charmed, still so easily charmed, by the 7 train and her pretty little neighborhood.

Especially in the spring. A profusion of azaleas, lilacs, daffodils, tulips, and pansies. The little square balconies on some of the row houses came to life with freshly potted flowers and tables and chairs set out. The playgrounds grew fuller with children playing, running, laughing. There was more vibrant life here than she had expected.

Summer was intoxicating, with bright pink roses, purple and blue hydrangeas, and thick clumps of tall white and purple phlox. Scents of honeysuckle and gardenias perfuming whole streets. More people strolling in the evenings, more bicyclists and joggers, more people tending their gardens.

In the fall, the streets were lined with trees of yellow and red, their leaves ending up in piles to be kicked through on Honora's walks. Pumpkins and chrysanthemums appeared in the tiny yards, and the houses with families went all out for Halloween. As they did for Christmas, with tiny lights glowing through the snow. The winter snowfalls outlined all the bare tree limbs in white and settled on the sloping slate roofs. Snug, cozy, the scent of wood fires lingering in the air.

At night, at the first hint of dusk, Honora made it a ritual to turn on the small leafy lamp she had bought while visiting her sister in Seattle. A torchiere with bronze vines and leaves twining up the amber glass, its light all soft and golden. Perfect for nights when she sat at her table to write, gazing out at the night sky and the neighborhood lights.

On one such winter afternoon, with the snow falling heavily outside the windows, she fixed a cup of tea, and began to work on the fairytale that she had begun back at her Manhattan apartment. The story had stayed with her, developing during her many walks, and she had jotted down bits and pieces, imagery, conversations, scenes. She was now ready to complete it. How perfect that there was a near blizzard outside her window, allowing her easy access into the snowy world of her story.

The Golden Blanket

In a northern kingdom, long ago and far away, there lived a king, a queen, and a princess who was just entering womanhood. Ever since the princess was a little girl, she had radiated warmth and love and sunshine. However, at night, she always grew cold. And the older she became, the colder she became.

When the princess was a little girl, the queen slept with her at night to keep her warm, wrapping her arms tightly around her. But every morning the queen awoke with a powerful (and unqueenly) sneezing cold (a-ah-AHH-CHOOOA!), and the king finally forbade her to sleep with the princess.

The king and queen tried placing the princess's kittens in bed with her, but one by one they left during the night. In the morning they were found curled up in front of the fireplace. When their simple attempts to keep her warm repeatedly failed, they consulted all the ministers and counselors, all the wise women and magicians, all the medicine people, and all the most learned of their kingdom.

However, the princess's unusual condition baffled every one of them, though many remedies were tried. Hot stones were nestled beneath her covers at night. Layer upon layer of woolen and feather-stuffed blankets were heaped upon her until she was nearly crushed from their weight.

A second fireplace was added to her room. And then a third. And then another and another until she was surrounded by fireplaces. Yet in the morning her skin was like ice, her lips a cold blue color. The king and queen feared that if a solution could not be found, they would wake up one morning to an icicle princess.

In the early years, they were hopeful that their daughter would simply outgrow the condition. For when the first rays of sun crept through the leaded windows, even the pale winter sun, the princess began to thaw.

Upon rising, she would sit in front of the window and gaze at the frost flowers on the glass and the snowy world outside. In the brief warm season, she would open her windows to blossoms and leaves. Then slowly she became warm and happy and animated, scarcely remembering the cold of night.

But year by year, it was taking her longer and longer and longer to thaw. The princess noticed that even her dreams were beginning to freeze. She used to dream of the busy marketplace, or the village children playing games, or meadow flowers dancing in the breeze. But now she dreamed of vast frozen landscapes, still and white and silent.

In the spring, the queen sat on her throne, watching her daughter frolic with the other young girls, gathering flowers and singing. For a few fleeting hours, the princess was able to enjoy the warmth of the day.

"Next winter will be her sixteenth birthday. I fear – I fear . . ." The queen could not finish her thought.

A sad nod from the king. "That if a solution is not found, it will be her last."

He pounded his hand on the arm of his throne. "We must act!"

The queen rose to her feet. "Indeed, we must!" She waited for him to speak.

"I – I will send out a proclamation!"

"Far and wide!" added the queen.

"A great reward will be given to the person who can solve the problem of our slowly freezing princess."

After consulting with the court counsel, it was decided that in three months, beginning with the summer solstice and lasting for the entire summer, a festival would be held such as no one had ever seen. At the heart of the festival, a competition would be held to solve the icy problem. Prizes would be given to all worthy contestants. If anyone succeeded, the king would present them with land and fine steeds, and the queen would bestow on them gold and jewels. And fine clothing and lace and tiaras and exquisite embroidered fabric and anything else anyone wanted.

The day of the great festival arrived. Most of the guests traveled to the court in magnificent carriages and wondrous coaches. Others came on horseback, on camels, and a few even rode in on elephants. And a great many simply arrived on foot.

The courtyard fluttered with colorful tents. Flowers of every hue hung in garlands from pole to pole and around all the windows and doors. Bells and music and singing filled the air day and night. Long rows of stalls sold hearty food and fragrant drinks. Booths offered rich fabrics, exotic spices, perfumes, and oils. Vendors sold bowls and jars, shoes and stockings, hats and fans. Actors performed skits, puppeteers dazzled the children, minstrels sang, jugglers juggled colorful balls, and fortune tellers and palm readers doled out advice and hope. The marketplace bustled with buying and trading, laughter and applause, dancing and singing.

In the daytime, the princess wandered among the crowds and joined in the merrymaking, marveling at the people who came from faraway places. But as night approached, she slowed down as the cold began to creep into her. She wasn't able to participate in the night activities, which were the most beautiful part of the festival, with the entire village lit up by bonfires and hundreds of candles and lanterns. Even though it was high summer, the princess bundled up in her purple velvet cloak and boots and watched the night festivities from the palace windows.

On every day of the summer-long festival, the king and queen sat upon their thrones on a high stage built for the presentation of remedy offerings. The princess sat between her parents, reveling in the excitement of the fair and grateful to all who brought possible solutions.

Representatives attended from all the neighboring lands, and many traveled from distant kingdoms. One after another, they presented their remedies: recipes for hot drinks, sure to warm the blood. Hot baths to be taken with crushed flowers and powdered roots. There were special warming herbs and oils and tonics. Magnificent blankets, thick and wooly. Magical stones purported to retain heat for days. And secret warming spells written on parchment scrolls.

The king and queen were hopeful. They were sure that one, if not many, of these solutions would warm their daughter. How could they not? To each person they gave a small bag of gold coins and their deepest thanks.

Each night, some of the solutions were tried. And each morning, the king and queen awoke to a pale blue princess. As the festival drew to a close, they grew downcast and began to lose hope.

They sat on their thrones in the final week, and with tears in their eyes they watched thin golden leaves drift from the trees. Autumn was approaching early in the northern kingdom. Winter was not far away.

On the last day of the offerings, a curiously attired man and woman approached the stage. They wore glittery turbans and slippers that turned up at the toes. Their flowing robes shimmered in shades of green, blue, and pink, and were embroidered with golden suns. They carried between them a small wooden chest studded with sparkling green, blue, and pink stones and inlaid with golden suns. The princess leaned forward in her throne, enthralled.

The crowd grew silent as the couple approached the stage and set the chest before the princess. Then they smiled at her, swept a gracious bow, and walked backwards as the curious crowd closed in around them.

"Wait!" called the king. "Your gold!"

"What are your names? Who sent you? Where do you come from?" cried the queen, her eyes searching for them in the crowd.

But the exotic emissaries seemed to have vanished. The throng pressed close to the stage to see what was in the chest. The queen unfastened the latch, the king raised the lid, and the queen lifted out – another blanket. Disappointment filled their faces, and tears rolled down the queen's cheeks.

The crowd groaned in disappointment. True, the blanket was beautiful – a soft, silky gold fabric, delicately embroidered with gold-threaded suns and white seed pearls. But it was thin, almost transparent, and not at all warm looking.

The princess, however, was enamored. She stepped forward and gently lifted the blanket. When she draped it open, a slip of paper fluttered out and fell to the ground. She opened the note and read:

"Sweet dreams, Princess."

It made her laugh, and she wrapped the blanket around her shoulders.

The king and queen linked hands and smiled sadly. "If it makes her happy, it is a good gift."

The festival drew to a close and the guests began to depart. The ministers and palace healers gathered the remaining remedies and placed them in the castle chamber where shelves had been built to house them. The sheer number promised hope, and every night one or two or more remedies were tried.

Autumn began to deepen. The flowers faded, and the green grasses turned brown. In the princess's chamber, a second fireplace was lit.

Then the mornings became silver with frost, and the sunlight thinned. A third fireplace was lit.

Every day, gift cures were brought in for the princess to try, but none of them worked. The nights grew longer and colder. The skies became heavy, and a cold bite entered the northern wind. A fourth fireplace was lit.

Winter drew closer and closer. When the first snow-flakes rode in on the wind, the remaining fireplaces were lit in the princess's bedroom. The heavy snowstorms were now upon them. While other children went on sleigh rides and skated and made snow castles, the princess huddled close to the fireplaces.

More remedies were tried, more remedies failed. The days grew shorter, and the princess grew bluer. It looked as if this would indeed be the princess's last winter.

The king and queen were down to the last pile of offerings. There were only a few more potions and roots and tonics. More heavy covers were piled upon the princess, and the stones baked in fire were placed in her bed. But it was taking the princess longer and longer and longer to thaw out in the morning.

One evening, the wizards and ministers, councilors, and wise women gathered around the princess's bed, wringing their hands and arguing over what should be done. The princess murmured a few halting words.

"Hush!" said the queen. "The princess speaks."

Through stiff, numb lips, the princess said, "The golden blanket – bring me the golden blanket."

The king was about to object. What could a thin blanket do that the thick blankets could not? The bearded councilors agreed with him, but the queen said, "Let her try it. What harm can it do?"

The king shrugged, and the chest was brought from the hall that was now full of discarded gifts. They draped the thin golden blanket on top of the princess. Then they reached for the other coverings and heaped them on top of her: thick woolen mantles, quilted cottons, fluffy eiderdowns, and heavy velvets, layering blanket upon blanket over the princess. They added logs to all the fireplaces and stoked the flames.

Then the king and queen kissed their daughter's cold blue cheeks. The ministers and wise women sadly shook their heads, and one by one they left the room.

As the princess lay cold and shivering beneath the blankets, near the doors of her ice sleep, a curious sensation ran through her. She tried to puzzle out what it was, but then the shivering stopped, and she immediately fell into a deep sleep.

In her sleep she began to dream. And in her dream strange, wondrous images filled her mind, warming her completely. She saw a shimmering golden green, heard a soft rustling, and saw the leaves and fronds of trees swaying in a gentle breeze. The air was full of golden particles of sunlight as she slept on soft, fragrant green grass. New sounds of birdsong drifted around her, and it seemed that someone caressed her hair as she lay sleeping. That was her dream.

In the morning, the king and queen slowly cracked opened the door to the princess's bedroom, fearful of what they would find – and were astounded! All the bedspreads and quilts and mantles and eiderdowns were thrown off the bed – except for the thin golden blanket. And the princess was smiling in her sleep. Her cheeks were rosy and her lips were pink. They hadn't seen her look so glowing since she was a tiny child.

She opened her eyes and nestled under the blanket, smiling at her parents. "I am warm. I dreamed of golden green in a beautiful land."

The king and queen embraced each other. "A reward!" shouted the king.

"A reward for the man and woman who brought the golden blanket!" said the queen.

But when they tried to find them, they could not. No one knew from which kingdom or land they had come. The king and queen tried to trace them by having their ministers question everyone who had attended the festival.

"I saw them leave on an elephant," one man said.

"No, it was on a camel," said someone else.

"It was a painted caravan they left in."

"No, a flying carpet," said yet another.

And still others said they had simply left on foot. It seemed that they left at various times, in various directions, by various means.

On the second night, logs were piled in the fireplaces and all the blankets were carted in. The princess insisted she didn't need them, but the fires were lit and the bedspreads layered upon her. As soon as she was alone, however, she doused the fires and kicked off the covers, leaving only the golden blanket. And she sank into a warm, deep sleep.

That night she dreamed of sparkling golden blue. She heard a soft roar, a rhythmic crashing, and realized that she was near an ocean, a thing she had only heard of in tales. She was sleeping in a billowing tent, striped blue, white, and gold, and listening to the soft lapping of waves, and dreaming of glittering golden sand and shimmering blue waves. Again, it seemed to her that someone caressed her hair as she slept.

In the morning, the king and queen peeked around the door, hoping to find their daughter warm and glowing again.

"I am warm," the princess said on waking. "I dreamed of golden blue in a beautiful land."

The king sent out notices throughout the kingdom, trying to find any information about the gift bearers who had brought the golden blanket. "Surely they will come back to claim their reward," he said.

On the third night, no fires were lit, and the heavy blankets were left outside the princess's room. Though a heavy snow fell outside her window, she slept with just the golden blanket and was warm.

In her dream, she was once again in a sun-filled land. Golden light shone on fragrant pink flowers in the garden where she slept. Nearby, a small pond sparkled with sunlight, and bright pink flowers floated on the water.

As she lay asleep in her dream, she suddenly thought, "Why am I sleeping in such a beautiful place? Let me awaken and explore this golden land."

She opened her eyes and saw the pink flowers in the garden, the rustling golden green leaves above, and the shimmering blue ocean in the distance – everything glimmered in golden sunlight.

The princess stood and gazed all about her, deeply breathing in the beauty. She then wandered around the garden, delighting in the soft balmy breeze, the vibrant colors and rich fragrances of the flowers and shrubs and trees. She beheld a large palace filled with balconies and wide verandas, all blooming with flowers and blossoming trees, everything tinged with the gold of the sun.

She felt that she was seeking something, longing for something, and she let this feeling guide her. It led her down a path along a warm stone wall with flowering vines, and she realized that she was within the palace garden. She passed white peacocks drinking from reflecting pools, and small white songbirds splashing in the fountains.

Then she saw a magnificent flowering white tree in the center of the garden and walked towards it. She raised her face to its blossoms, inhaling their delicate scent, and ran her hand along the smooth bark.

The princess hesitated when she noticed the edge of a woven mat on the other side of the tree. She slowly peered around the trunk, gasping in delight at what she saw. There was a golden foot, and then a white robed figure, and then the head of a peacefully sleeping youth.

She stepped closer to behold the beautiful lad. His hair was black and curly, his skin golden. She kneeled beside him and reached out her hand to stroke his hair.

At that moment he opened his eyes. Beautiful eyes that looked both fierce and gentle. She backed up, but he smiled.

"You have come at last," he said. "Long have I dreamed of you in your cold winter land. Your cool dream breezes have come to me. You have kept the heat and fever away from me. My beautiful princess: finally, I awake to you."

"It was you who sent me the golden blanket!" the princess said. "You kept me warm and saved me from the cold."

Then, hand in hand, they strolled through the golden land. The more she saw, the more enchanted she became with the prince and his land. He walked her through the gardens full of pink flowers, the groves of shimmery green trees, the soft sands and blue ocean, and – and then, she woke up.

Every morning the princess awoke, disappointed to be back in the cold northern kingdom. And every night she dreamed of the prince, the gardens, the groves, the ocean. She was seeing new colors, hearing new sounds, smelling new fragrances, all with the warm gold of the sun in them. In her dream, the prince and princess wanted to marry and live together forever.

The princess told her parents of the youth who gave her the golden blanket, and she described his beautiful land. She explained that without him, she was frozen, and without her, he was locked in a sleeping fever.

She told them that he was coming to marry her and take her back to his kingdom where she could thrive. The king and queen were eager to thank the person who was responsible for saving their daughter.

On the first day of the next summer solstice festival, the same exotic emissaries arrived again, this time followed by the young prince and the king and queen of a southern kingdom. The northern king and queen welcomed them to their land.

The southern king and queen said: "Our prince was in a fever, and only cooled at night when he dreamed of the princess. Truly they were meant to be together."

The northern king and queen said: "Our princess was beginning to freeze. The prince and his golden blanket and sweet dreams saved our daughter. Truly they were meant to be together."

The prince and princess were married at the end of the summer festival, and then they journeyed to the golden land. They lived half of their time in the north when it was mild, and half in the southern kingdom. Their days were filled with golden happiness and love.

And the princess was never cold again.

The End

Honora sent "The Golden Blanket" and other stories to publishing houses, adding to the slush piles of Manhattan. Her "submitted" file, along with the file for rejection letters, was growing satisfyingly larger. Satisfying, because it meant that her chances were increasing (*"if you throw enough spaghetti,"* said Honey), and that, hopefully, her writing was improving. (Nora gazed at the file and muttered, *"Too much optimism can be dangerous."*)

Wanting to use her degree in some way (Nora's idea), and wanting to become a part of her beloved neighborhood (Honey's idea), Honora looked around for opportunities. She decided that she would enjoy volunteering at a local community center, helping immigrant children with English by reading stories to a small group on Saturdays.

She got to know their parents and siblings, and listened to their stories, their bravery, their dreams – talk about

STORY: high stakes, drama, extreme character arcs, long-ing and loss, struggle and conflict, the suspense of unknown endings, the unexpected, the archetypes! *They're living the thing I'm trying to create on paper. Humbling.*

There still remained that pesky problem of money. The income from her job at a local coffee shop barely covered rent and she was dipping into her meager savings. The idea popped into Honora's mind that perhaps she should become an ESL tutor. Teaching "English as a Second Language" would utilize her degree (sort of), had a practical ring to it (sort of), and would answer her longing to travel (in a sort of a reversed kind of way). After all, how hard could it be to teach English? she asked herself, ignoring her attempts to learn other languages.

She devoted her time to a course on teaching ESL and took on a brief tutoring stint to test the waters. Brief, because she soon sank. She fretted over her first tutoring assign-ments and feared that she was making things worse for her students.

As with the young man who asked for help pronouncing the world "develop." He said no one could understand him when he used that word at his job. He grew increasingly frustrated as Honora tried to help him, using her hands, her arms, and volume to help explain her words – "put the emphasis on the SECOND syllable, De VEL op." She gave an encouraging punch to the air with each of his attempts: "Dvlp, dvlep, devlep."

Then there was grammar and the confused expressions and the logical questions for which there were no logical answers:

"So why you say 'Aren't I?' but not 'I are?'"

"Why not 'I have two childrens?'"

"How come 'I went' but not 'I didn't went?'"

"Why I can say 'I like,' but not 'I no like?'"

Yeah, Honora wondered. *Why bring in "do?" I go, but, I do not go. Too wordy.* She was tempted to tell them to go ahead and say it their way, that it did make more sense. "I don't, you don't, he don't." Far more logical. She was tempted to start speaking like that herself. *I no go.*

After a particularly tangled lesson on the *third person singular "s,"* Honora gave up the idea of a career in ESL teaching. (For once, Nora and Honey were in agreement.) She could still volunteer at the center and read stories to the children, but, like her students, she was daunted by the inconsistencies of English grammar, and doubted her ability to teach. And as far as making enough money to pay the rent? Perhaps it was time to try temping. (Nora perked up at the practical solution. Honey protested, *"Don't expect me to wear a suit."*)

Honora practiced on her new laptop that she bought for writing stories and worked on increasing her typing speed and learning the mandatory trio Word/Excel/PowerPoint. She sat in drab rooms at various temp agencies where she was tested (humiliating somehow) and soon had her first assignment.

And so began the period of temping and the oh-so-tentative step into the corporate world (prison bars!) and taking the 7 train into Manhattan.

It was relatively simple to get into the city and transfer to the other lines at Lexington or Times Square, though there were a few initial mishaps and late arrivals. And if Honora didn't pay close attention on the return trip, she ended up in Astoria.

Riding the train everyday was an experience in itself. She had been able to walk to most of her waitressing jobs in the city. This rush-hour subway world was eye-opening. Always different. So many people pressed so closely together, with the invisible personal-space barrier paper thin between them.

She watched nervously at the young women applying makeup. Blush, okay. Lipstick, a little trickier but still, okay. But mascara! Far too dangerous, wasn't it? The first few times she observed it, she held her breath, waiting for a scream, or at least a smear, when the train lurched around a curve. But those women didn't even blink. They continued to keep their eyes wide open as they glanced in the compact mirror – ignoring the swaying train, and the stares from children and gawking adults, like herself.

There were the women who knitted and crocheted, calmly lengthening their rows of stitches and lace. And, of course, there were the readers. Newspapers and crossword puzzles, magazines and books. Honora would surreptitiously crane her neck to see the book covers, trying to match the reader to a genre.

And there were the sleepers. In the mornings some of them even snored, as if they were still in their warm beds at home.

And there were many others who stared blankly out the windows or at the floor, lost in thought, or lost in not thinking at all. It was hard to tell. (*"I can tell,"* said Honey, still resisting the new career direction. *"They're bored."*)

Honora began adding entries into her notebook just for the 7 train.

> "The Train of Hope." You get in the crowded subway car and observe all the individual people (very few couples or people who seem to know one another). The woman holding onto the pole with one hand, her other hand holding a book. On the cover is a picture of a man and woman kissing. The hope of love and romance.
>
> I bump into what I think is another book or magazine when the train takes a curve and rocks me backwards. I turn around to see that it's a man scratching off a lottery ticket. The hope of a windfall.

Everyone greeting the day with hope that today is going to get them one step closer to their dreams, a better future. The Future is the carrot that dangles in front of us. Just there, ahead of us, are all the wonderful things life might have in store for us, if we can just keep inching towards it.

The ads on the train foster such hope. Cynics might say it's false hope, but an optimist would say hope is hope. For example, the ads for careers in fashion design and mixing music, or a promising career by going to this college or that vocational school. Mattress ads for deeper sleep, ads for clearer skin, shinier hair, and her favorite, the school ad for philosophy! How abstract. How do you advertise for courses in philosophy? You state that everything else fades or is risky and could disappear in a moment's blink – beauty, sound sleep, money, jobs, relationships. But philosophy lasts through life. More hope.

The young couple, his head on her shoulder, laughing. A child's singing coming from the back, signs and sounds of happiness. Hope is happiness. It's the dream that makes us wake in the morning, ready to join the struggle, offering us one more crack at life.

The train picks up speed in the tunnel, the light of morning temporarily blacked out. Soon to surface in the bustling, hope-and-dream-filled city.

Honora entered New York City's temp pool. She filled in for the people who called in sick, for women on maternity leave, the last-minute call-outs, the people on vacation, the workers who couldn't take it one more day and quit (was that an act of hope? Or desperation?). She was the stop-gap while the company searched for a "real" employee.

There were several good things about these one-or-two-day fill-ins, or week-long assignments. She got a sense of different industries, different areas of the city, different people. Plus, as there was frequently downtime, she could type some of her writings, or jot down ideas. These jobs made sense for now. Eventually, she took on some of the longer positions, and once or twice, tried out a few temp-to-perm possibilities.

And yet, after several months, Honora noticed a certain dullness creeping into her life, and the trains didn't seem so full of hope anymore. Was it the routine? The lack of meaning in the work itself? (*"Yes,"* answered Honey. Nora countered in a resigned manner, *"It pays the rent."*) And the rudeness she now often saw on the trains? Had it always been there?

Honora tried to amuse herself on the train rides, reading books, or magazine articles.

> So now they're saying that Neanderthals and other hominids likely died out because of a supervolcano. There's a lake in Indonesia that seems to prove it. Makes sense. Of course, every explanation regarding life makes sense because life itself is so astounding and makes no sense whatsoever.

> It wasn't that long ago they said that Neanderthals probably died out because they didn't plan ahead (I had felt such an affinity with them and was sure I had inherited some "live for today, don't worry about tomorrow" Neanderthal DNA).

And before that, they were saying that *Homo sapiens* probably wiped out the Neanderthals. (That also made sense. Just look around.)

Now it would seem that we – our species – barely survived at all. That at one point, we were probably reduced to about 5,000 people, the size of my hometown. We just barely made it onto the world's stage. It's so amazing that I just accept it. I feel like I should do something about it. Throw a party for humanity, celebrate the near miss.

(*"Yeah, we could do that,"* Nora replied in a lackluster tone.)

Honora attempted to write and create, calling on Honey for inspiration and Nora for perseverance. But her output was lessening, there was no denying it.

Forcing herself to write over her lunchbreak, she jotted down thoughts from her morning commute. *Here's one for you, Nora*, Honora offered.

"Skeletons everywhere." Warmer weather reveals the T-shirts and pendants and tattoos of skulls that so many high school and college students wear. What is it about skeletons that so enamors a certain age group? On the subways, in parks, and on city streets, you can always find a teen, usually male, wearing a skeleton image. The girls go more for the Goth look – *I'm alive, but I look dead.*

As they get a little older, the images shrink – instead of a pharaoh skeleton emblazoned in sequins on a jacket, they are scaled down to a print made of tiny skulls, a skeleton T-shirt, or perhaps a simple ring. What is the message they are trying to give – *I am in easy company with death and dying and all things dark and fearful and macabre.* It's a safe attitude to have when you're young.

Imagine a 90-year-old Goth woman or a 100-year-old guy wearing a shirt with a skull. Now that would be really creepy – and somewhat redundant.

A smile crept over Honora's lips. *I'm going to have to remember to do that.*

("*Uh-huh.*" Nora put her chin in her hand, bored. Honora looked around, almost desperately, for Honey. *Where has*

Honey gone off to? Nora replied with a wave of her hand. *"Off flitting around the fairysphere."*)

❦

Honora sighed. Instead of the laser focus on writing, she found that her mind wandered more, drifting, unmoored. Was she beginning to resemble the people on the train who stared blankly at the floor or out the windows? She began to notice subtle shifts in herself.

Like when she waited on the station platform. She would look around, check the sky for clouds or colors, and haphazardly follow the musings of her mind. She would make out the clear disc of the sun obscured by cloud cover, so like a full moon, and wonder – Is it just a weird coincidence that the sun and the moon appear to be the same size?

(*"Maybe,"* answered Honey) but Honora could tell she wasn't really interested.

Or she would follow a meandering linguistic thread in her mind: Here's a curious thing. The words "good" and "evil" are only one letter away from "god" and "devil." Is that a coincidence? Are there other words like that? Are there answers for everything? What would that philosophy course have to say about that?

(*"My guess: Not much,"* answered Nora.)

Or standing in a crowded morning rush-hour train, heading over the Sunnyside train yard, Honora would stare at signs and advertisements in the train, and, Scrabble-like, try to make words. How many words could she find in DO NOT LEAN ON DOOR? Elan, odor, drool . . .

(No comment whatsoever from either Nora or Honey. She couldn't blame them.)

Or staring out the window, over drab Long Island City, she would call upon her old habit of finding spots of beauty. They were usually to be found in the sky, rather than in the buildings – though the old church steeple seen from the 33rd Street station could always be counted on. Its spire reminded her of one in a Breughel painting – the harvest one? Or was it the peasant dance?

Honora looked at the high school building, and the steeple in the distance, and imagined dates posted in the sky next to them, like thought bubbles or tiny post-its. The boxy, aqua-toned school had a "1960" posted above its flat roof. The Breughel-like steeple had "1391" hovering near it. She scanned the view for another age from deeper time, but found nothing. Then she decided that if the church steeple could be Breughel, then that smokestack could be "1850." Manchester. Industrial Age. The buildings with the Art Deco trim, a "1932." The Long Island City landscape became dotted with little date posts – until the train plunged down into the darkness of the tunnel.

She eventually grew tired of that bit of entertainment and developed a different game. On her daily rides into the city, as she waited at the elevated station for the flying trains (that didn't look so magical in the early morning), she would search for beauty in the sky and try to put it into words. Her old friend the sky. She took to calling the game "The Sky Today." (*"That's better,"* said Honey.)

It was a late-July sky, a morning sky with high white clouds. (*"Boring! Specifics!"* chided Nora. *"What kind of a writer are you?"*)

The morning sky was a mix of horizontal and round clouds – as if someone were wearing stripes and polka dots. An odd mix. (Honey tilted her head, in doubtful consideration.)

Low layers of clouds on the horizon, a sheen of silvery gold and deep blue-gray. Above those clouds, puffy rounded clouds with those same two tones, the gray all at the bottoms of the clouds, and on one side there were kind of these purplish . . . She could go on indefinitely with wordy descriptions since the sky was always shifting. Sometimes she was grateful to see the train arriving. (So were Nora and Honey.)

It was true that the 7 train ride that links Queens to Manhattan was beautiful at night. In the daylight, however, it wasn't so pretty. Heading into the city, once the train sailed by the Tudor-style apartment buildings of Sunnyside, it passed over the rundown warehouses of Long Island City which are bleak and depressing in all weather. It's the same for Manhattan. Except for small pockets, much of the city is dreary. You really had to know where to look. And remember to wear your rose-tinted glasses.

Honora was glad when her nieces and nephews visited, like the old days when her brothers and sisters used to visit. She played tour guide and fell in love with the city anew. And how thrilling that her niece was going to study in Milan! Over dinner they made plans for Honora to visit. Perhaps her traveling days would finally begin. A recent postcard from her traveling uncle – postmarked Samarkand! – stoked her longing for faraway places.

Another year had passed. Winter again. What had she accomplished – a few drafts, one piece sent to an agent? Pathetic.

Honora noticed an old man on the rush hour Sunnyside subway platform. *Still going to work?* she worried – *at his age?* She observed him during the ride, and when his weary face broke into a smile, Honora also smiled and followed his gaze.

He was looking out the window, watching birds flying in the snow. She imagined the world through his eyes, and made up a story about him. She jotted down her thoughts once she arrived at her desk.

"Old Man and Seagulls in Snow"

Another day, another dollar. I head to work in a heavy March snowstorm, making my way to the subway station. I pull myself up the stairs, my knees and hips stiff today – must be the cold.

I start my trek into town above ground. I'm always grateful that part of my train line is elevated and I can begin the day looking out over the neighborhoods. The train arrives, but is too crowded to get on. And the next train, packed like sardines, flies by us by altogether. A collective groan.

I wait in the storm for the next train. The wind blows hard up here on the platform. I pull my hat down and hug my chest. Thankfully, another train soon arrives, slows, stops. The doors open and I manage to squeeze in. There's an announcement to stand clear of the closing doors. They open and close a few times, and the conductor hollers over the loudspeaker: "Stop blocking the doors! Step inside!" The doors finally shut and the train heads to the next station.

I keep near the doors so that I can look out at the falling snow and the streets down below. Above the stores lining Queens Boulevard and against the brick apartment buildings, I am surprised to see two lone seagulls flying in the snowstorm. Shouldn't they be tucked away under a ledge somewhere?

I watch the birds as they arc and soar above the flat rooftops. What are those two rascals doing out in the snow? I give a little chuckle at their antics. I look out over the snowflake-filled sky, large thick flakes coming at me in the wind. And those two birds sailing through it all, keeping pace with the train as we move.

Suddenly, I have my answer. Those seagulls are out in the snowstorm for the sheer fun of it! There they are gliding down, curving up, catching snowflakes in their beaks, playing a game of trying to fly in between the falling snow. Look at them! For a moment I am up there with them, flying in the white stuff, exhilarating in the sharp wind, twisting my body, and blinking the flakes out of my eyes, wheee heeee! raising my face into the wonder of a winter day.

My view is abruptly blocked as we pull into the next station. We come to a stop. The doors open, more people crowd in, the conductor hollers, and I must move to the middle of the car where I can't see out the window. A few more stations and the train heads underground into darkness. We rumble under the East River, and soon we are in Manhattan.

I exit the train and make my way to the steps that will take me to my job. Yes, another day another dollar – but part of me is lighter and happier. I am better for having flown a bit with the seagulls in the snow.

Honora finished typing the story at her cubicle and read over the words. When the mail cart arrived, she delivered magazines, letters, and memos to the desk of this week's boss.

The windows of his corner office allowed her a brief view to the outside world. She snatched a glance at the falling snow and tried a whispered *wheee heeee!* to see if she could muster up any of that joy.

∝⤙

The classes continued, the writing continued, the commuting continued, and staring at the sky searching for beauty continued.

It was a celestial sky, light illuminating the clouds from behind. Shadings of deep gray, but nothing dark or ominous, all lightness and richness from softly edged clouds set against a pale blue sky. My heart lifts.

∝⤙

It was a Constable sky. High, scudding clouds dominating the sky. Majestic, yet serene – she could almost see the painter pausing with his brush in hand.

∝⤙

Another day, another dollar. Once the novelty wore off, the temp jobs grew ever more boring, more monotonous. They were either extremely stressful – "the meeting is in ten minutes! Make thirty copies of these reports!" (of different sizes of paper). Copiers jamming, running from floor to floor to find a working copy machine, finally locating one, only to see the "change cartridge" flash in the middle of the second copy. Selecting the wrong image for "staple" in upper right-hand corner – why was there never a staple remover when you needed one? she wondered, as she pried them loose with her fingernails. Running to the lobby for food deliveries for the never-ending lunch meetings . . . Such days left her drained, with no room for story lines or motivation to pen a description.

On the other end of the temp spectrum was the extremely boring. Achingly, crushingly boring. Chained to a desk with nothing to do but wait. Almost praying that the phone would ring. Even a wrong number would be welcome, a voice from the other side. The stunning impossibility that not even five minutes had passed since she last checked the time.

Sometimes, to cheer herself, and still identifying with Cinderella the scullery maid, Honora would hum a tune from the TV musical: "In my own little corner in my own little chair, I can be whatever I want to be . . ." *That* is the perfect temp song! she thought, and humming it soon became a way to inaugurate a new desk, a new job.

Since Honora was an eager worker and was determined to do her best, she was frequently offered (dreadful) positions. She politely turned them down, fearing entrapment, fearing a diminishment of spirit, the complete disappearance of her dreams.

She still groaned when she remembered the Executive Assistant who summoned her into the conference room. Honora had been busy on the phone, dealing with a wrong number. She tried to decipher the caller's question in Spanish asking to speak with Paco. Her face had lit up – here was a chance to use her meager high school Spanish. She proudly answered, "Paco no está aquí." (Honey was already envisioning a quick trip to Mexico, or perhaps Puerto Rico, the rain forest!)

But the next question threw Honora. She gathered that the person was now asking – well where is he, will he be back soon? She shook her head and used her ESL large gestures as she stumbled. "No. I mean – Paco no trabajar trabajo trabaja aquí," she said, pointing to her desk. The caller then wanted to know where Paco was now working and if she could give the new number. Honora put her hand up. "Wait. Attendez s'il vous – I mean – Uno momento, por favor." Honora covered the receiver, and asked her fellow cubicle dwellers – "Does anyone speak Spanish?"

A red-sleeved arm snatched the phone from her, and the EA barked into the phone, "Wrong number!" and slammed it down. And then to Honora, she said, "Come with me."

Honora followed her into the conference room, feeling mildly guilty, though she had no idea why. Surely it was okay to try to help someone on the other line . . .

The EA parked herself at the head of the table, crossed her stilettoed heels, leaned back in the chair – and smirked, as if hoping Honora would squirm.

What is this? thought Honora. *I'm a temp!*

"Don't worry," the EA said with a patronizing air. "You're not in trouble."

Honora nearly bolted out of her chair. *NOT IN TROUBLE?* she wanted to scream. *I've been killing myself at this stupid job, covering your mistakes, staying late for the boss who spends all his time doing online trading –*

"We want to offer you the position – full time, with benefits. You will report to me (*"fat chance!"* cried Nora), continue to support the VP as well as his director reports, coordinate their travel and submit their expense reports, file, fax, schedule meetings, answer calls before the third ring, tidy the pantry, restocktheexecuteasdkfjefaefglllaab-laaaaaaaaaaa . . ."

The gray mass of words poured from the EA's mouth. Endless days, weeks, months, years of a meaningless existence stretched out before Honora, as she listened in wide-eyed Kurtz-like existential revulsion: *The horror! The horror!*

The EA frowned, as she often did, at Honora's long flowing skirt, the vintage jewelry, the floral scarf; clothes suggestive of gardens and tearooms, strolls along the Rive Gauche . . .

The EA gave a quick tug to the sleeves of her red wool power suit. "Of course, you'll have to dress in a manner more aligned with corporate values."

(Honey's head snapped up at that – she shot a worried glace to Nora. After a quick mutual nod, Nora grabbed Honey by the arm, burst through the conference room window, and Peter Pan/Wendy-like, they sailed over lower Manhattan, making their escape.)

The next day, Honora contacted the temp agency and requested a different job. No more hedge funds or banking companies, Please! (In her mind she was on her knees, pleading, hands clasped to the heavens.)

After a variety of admin jobs in retail, cosmetics, not-for-profit, communications, insurance, real estate . . . Honora finally got her answer to what went on inside all those tall buildings of Manhattan: Meetings. Just meetings. She thanked her stars that she was on the periphery of the moneyed, colorless corporate world, where the gears of commerce churned and fortunes were made for people on the upper floors.

Usually, after a few weeks – sometimes days – it was time to move on. Let's try something else. Again. And again and again. Just like her ole Cinderella, moving from village to village, job to job. (*"Whatever happened to her?"* wondered Honey. Nora gave a firm nod. *"Yeah!! You completely left her hanging!!"* Honey groaned out a huff. *"Must you always add exclamation points, as if you're in a perpetual bad mood? They're like bongs to the head,"* she said, rubbing her temple.)

Working in downtown Manhattan, Honora would seek out places of beauty to spend her lunch hour. At Trinity Church, if the weather was mild, she would sit outside on the benches among the centuries-old tombstones and stroll along the sidewalks. On cold or rainy days, she would find a pew inside, and if she was lucky, there would be a noontime concert, usually a quartet or a piano. Sometimes she would be swept away by the beauty of the music, making it all but impossible to leave the etherealness and go back to a stale office to do someone's bidding.

At Midtown jobs, Honora fled (hairpins still flying) to Central Park, oftentimes the delight of seasonal changes causing her to wander too far ("Excuse me, how do I get out of the Ramble?" or "Which way is Fifth Avenue?"), barely making it back to her desk in time.

In colder weather, she ducked into the near-empty, museum-like churches and cathedrals, sitting quietly as she observed the stained-glass windows, the old-world carved wood and mosaics, the lingering incense. Followed by the clash of worlds as she left the sanctuaries and passed through the revolving doors of large, bustling lobbies with frenzied crowds.

Honora flipped through her notebook one night and again froze in existential horror – all the pages were filled with job-related entries. Meaningless temp jobs. Filing, copying, answering phones for stranger bosses. The jobs had taken over her life! NOOOOO!!!!!!!

Honora used her lunch hour to wander the Upper East Side streets, admiring the beautiful synagogues, the historic hotels, the bookstores and restaurants, the shop windows. She stepped into a café to warm up with a cappuccino. With her chin in her hand, she gazed out the window at the bustling sidewalks and teeming traffic and wondered what it would look like if everyone suddenly just gave up. If at the exact same moment everyone thought – "I can't do it anymore. I give up." She imagined the pedestrians coming to a halt and sitting, slump-shouldered, on the sidewalks. The bicyclists dropping their bikes and doing the same. The traffic coming to a standstill, the drivers hanging their heads in defeat. She took another sip and shook her head. Better to keep going. Better to keep trying.

It was a metamorphic sky, layer upon stony layer. The sky heavier than the earth, pressing down on the horizon, crushing the clouds into stern bands of charcoal and granite.

Ah! A magical, wonderful, much-needed, revitalizing trip to Italy and France, and the world became once again beautiful, fascinating, fulfilling. Visiting her niece in Milan, and then an old friend from school in Florence. Five days on her own in Paris, wandering, wandering. The rebirth of her spirit, the flow of writing, the excitement, the promise . . . The reluctant return trip home.

The day moon was out, sitting lightly in the high blue sky. Upside down, whimsical, without its significance in the night sky. As wispy as a cloud, and almost as meaningless and unnoticed.

Honora continued to stand in the middle of the subway platform and scan the sky. Sometimes people would glance up from their Starbucks coffee cups, follow her gaze to an empty sky, and resume their conversation or go back to listening to music or reading or scowling in the direction of the oncoming train wondering WHEN IT WOULD F!%(@Q!@*!#!* ARRIVE ALREADY?!!

Honora gazed out at a perfectly blue sky and felt uninspired. It was the kind of sky that made people happy, the kind of sky that people wrote songs about. Oddly enough, Honora never really cared for a perfectly blue sky. There was nothing in it to hang onto. It was flat, flat. She squinted into it, trying to delve into that pure shade of blue to find something. Peering, peering, but seeing only those squiggly clear shapes, blue on blue, that come from the retina or cones or some such place in the eyes, and making her think of eyeballs and mortality and other things that pulled her away from beauty.

She much preferred clouds, stormy skies, ripples of gray and gold, puffy shapes, and swirls of white. It gave her something to engage with, provided traction for her imagination. Her mind went slipping and sliding off the smooth surface of that porcelain blue sky.

Honora forced herself to sit at her kitchen table and write. After two hours, she had dutifully filled two pages with uninspired writing. The sun would set soon. She hurried out into the sunset world and breathed deeply of the summer dusk. Fireflies! Or as they called them in the Midwest, Lighting bugs! The little glows blinking on and off soothed her head with a fanciful bit of magic.

Another hard blue cloudless sky, a flat surface that she hit her forehead against. She wanted a textured sky, one with clouds, colors, moods, skies to figure out, to describe, skies full of interest and future. Something was sure to happen in those cloud-heavy skies – rain, snow, a storm, the colors changing. The blue sky held the eternal present, unchanging, unimaginative.

In the fall the sky filled – with bison! It was a herd of bison, all shoulders and downward-thrusting heads, stampeding. Clouds of swirling dust surrounding them as they charged forward into the western storm. Honora tipped her head. Something about that imagery sounded familiar. She was sure she had read a similar description somewhere over the years. Perhaps those rumbling roiling cumulonimbus clouds along the horizon often took the shape of buffalos?

Honora continued to take writing classes, rushing off after the temp jobs, and coming alive with a sense of purpose as she neared the schools, submitted pieces, commented on students' writings, and went out afterwards to cafés with a classmate or two to discuss ideas, or just to sip on hot chocolate together.

She sent pieces to publishing houses, searched for an agent, began another file for rejection letters, entered contests, and eagerly checked the mailbox on her way home from work to see if she had won. This writing business was harder than it looked. She was growing tired of always seeking approval from a nameless, faceless person in the industry.

Only her walks and her writing connected her with the world she longed for. (Honey held up one of the long skirts, matching it to a sweater. *You left out music, and books, and museum visits, lamplights in the dusk, and scented baths. Cozy cafés, candlelight, street fairs . . .*)

Sometimes Honey's unflappability was exhausting.

"The dream is always most beautiful before it ever begins." – HG

The pages of the notebook filled. She wrote about him in her other books. But the thought of him spilled over into everything she wrote. And did. And thought. And dreamed. Yet their paths in life were diverging, not converging.

A grueling two-month assignment in the executive offices of a Fortune 500 Company (woo. hoo.) that felt like two years. She needed a vacation. Travel to some faraway place. But she didn't have paid time off for such luxuries. Was it time to consider a "real" job where she would have such benefits? (Honey glanced out the window and pretended not to hear the appalling question, but Nora had to point out, "*Well, if you would have listened to me years ago . . .*")

Train. Work. Train. Home. Train. Work. Train. Home. Train Delay. Work. Home. Train.

From the train window to the west, the sky hung in low, churning clouds. Bands of gray, like waves on an immense sky ocean but inverted, seen from underneath. Honora was below the waves, being rolled and tumbled in the turbulent ocean off a distant shore. She almost felt a little seasick being tossed about in the underwater world.

It was a crossroads sky – long paths of gray-blue clouds, roads with deep ruby ruts, edged in the silvery white of dust. Long bands crossing the sky, thinner roads cutting diagonally across them – a sky full of roads, paths, directions, possibilities.

"Her Last Hour"

It was the image of herself as an old woman. How she imagined herself in the last hour of her life. Forty years from now, perhaps fifty. Like a picture, an old miniature painted in rich colors that she was the subject of.

In this picture, she was alone in a garden-like room. It was late afternoon and the sun streamed into the room from the window on her right, warming the room and filling the air with the tiniest particles of golden light. In her lap, a book rested, face down. Her wispy gray hair was swept up. Her dress was long and loose, patterned with blue and white flowers. And in the room, flowers in the corners, on the window ledge, in terra cotta pots – pink, red, purple. Plants she had taken care of for many years.

From deep inside where the golden particles had warmed her, and the books and people and all the long years had filled her, a feeling began to stir and release itself. Everything was even and calm now. She had lived the life she wanted. And now she was gently rocking, nearly asleep. Yes. Warm and surrounded, she gave a faint smile, in agreement that it was now time to go, her death breath spiraling upwards.

She often imagined her death like that. A gentle fading away or into something. No gripping thought at the end of: No! that is not what I meant! I meant to live a different sort of life – full, expanding, enriching.

There would not be that thought at the end of her life. She would do whatever it took to become her true self. She carried her death image loosely around her neck like a pendant. And when the city became too harsh, love too oppressive, time too constrictive, she would pull out the pendant and gaze at it, saying all this other will pass. Do not give in. Do not compromise. There is a room of warm golden light awaiting you at the end.

(Nora felt bad as she watched Honey blink away tears at the conclusion that was meant to be comforting, but wasn't.)

From the train window, Honora gazed at the misty horizon. The sky, a low purple-blue bank with magician's smoke curling above it. Wisps like gauze. Smokey veils obscuring who knows what realms of wonder. A pale silver shimmers through the veil. Below on the street level, glittery golden headlights from the boulevard speak of their own magical realms.

(Nora raised one eyebrow. *"Magical, glittering, golden? It seems to me you haven't moved on much. Your writing remains much the same."* Honey tried a gentler touch. *"Perhaps it's time to continue that story. About the dream pearls."*) "Yeah. Maybe," said Honora.

Getting on the 7 train. First, there is the rush and push and pigeons and spit of the platforms. Then comes the crunch of elbows and backpacks, the tinny iPod sounds from every direction, the onslaught of overpowering fragrance (a.m.) or sweat (p.m.), someone eating neon-orange cheese curls and holding the same pole as you are with their sticky fingers that get licked clean now and then, the weight of the day hanging like a heavy backpack on the journey back home. Honora thinks, *God, this is a hard city. How long can I do this? How long before my knees won't take the stairs anymore, my tolerance won't take the indifference, the rudeness?*

Then, in the midst of all that awful drag pulling her down, down, down – there it is – the lifting strains of a cello across the platform, or the ethereal sound of a violin threading the air with the pure gold of some melody you recognize and love, or strange, beautiful sounds from an unknown African or Asian instrument, or a lone voice. Some artist who braves it all – the indifferent crowds, the noisy trains that drown out their music, the coins or dollars or smiles that may or may not be given – There it is. The beauty that keeps her glued to this city. The shocking, unexpected blessing of a gift given, richness bestowed, the beauty of humanity shining through the squalor.

"The Immigrants' Song"

A tired Honora took the subway home, a bruised spirit from a bruised day. Lucky to have found a seat, though disappointed that it was next to two guitar-strumming, poncho-wearing musicians. *I just want peace and quiet*, she thought. *Oh well. Maybe they will drown out all the harshness of the day.*

She had listened to generic others, who sometimes seemed to be strumming the same chord through the entire song, or the older accordion players. She had listened to – and admired – the spirit that keeps trying, that lives on hope, those determined strugglers who work for their money. Usually one song per car – "Cielito Lindo," "La Vie en Rose," or something familiar – the quick hat pass, a dash out the door and into the next car before the doors close.

Unless, like today, the musicians began to sing at the beginning of the tunnel. It would mean more songs.

As they began to perform, she noticed that the musicians were two older men. One with a guitar, one with some kind of wheel-like instrument holding several harmonicas. What were the plaintive, evocative melodies they sang? Her high school Spanish caught a few words now and then – *vida, mi corazon, yo quiero* . . . songs of love and life. They tugged at her, those foreign words and melodies, finding recognition in the part of her that understood the part of them that was singing those songs.

Then, most poignantly, and the last song before her stop, one of them sang a song in English, so heavily accented that she almost couldn't understand – "Sone tine I fee lugga moder less chile." Ah. Understanding graced and honored the beautiful melody – "Sometimes I feel like a motherless child, far far away from home." The haunting spiritual still voicing human bitterness, loss, sadness, separation. Now in a different time, a different people. For all of us far away from the home of our youth, from the quiet strength of mother love that nothing else will ever compare to, to the aloneness in the midst of our crowded lives, or perhaps like these musicians, in a foreign country.

Along with a few others, she pulled out a dollar and dropped it in his hat. Some people didn't even hear the song because of their iPods. Others had learned to close their ears and eyes as a form of protective isolation.

She thought the words were made more beautiful by being broken, words from a grown man, far far from home. A song from the past, given another meaning for these immigrants, and to some degree, even for her. Our homelands, our pasts, that we are forever trying to capture and shape into words, melodies, colors – elusive, often sad, and always far more beautiful than they ever really were.

It was another Constable sky – all drama and portent high up in the sky, only touching earth on the far horizon, not enough to disturb the gentle tranquility of the land.

Honora observed the people on the train on her way home from her latest class. That beautiful mix of people from all over the world. Sometimes she would fix on a figure, a face, and wonder what their story was. Where were they from? What were their lives like? Did they miss their homeland? Did they dream of it at night?

She glanced down at the notes she had taken from tonight's class. She was enjoying the short story class, the possibilities of the form, its flexibility. She mentally listed all the writing classes she had taken over the years: playwriting, children's writing, screenwriting, novel writing, poetry.

Years of classes, she thought with a slight, worried wince. Time is passing. I really should settle on one or two forms.

A marbled paper sky. Blue-gray and pale-pink whorls swirling into a deeper gray sky, darker strips of marbled sky rolling in from some northern front. A fluid blossoming of pinks and blues.

The Would-Be Princess and her Dream Pearls

Once upon a time there lived a beautiful princess in a wondrous kingdom (*"Like the teacher said, 'Scrap the adjectives,'"* bossed Nora. *"Out of the way,"* said Honey. *"Let the muse flow through her."*)

She wasn't actually literally a princess, though she probably would have been in another time and place and under different circumstances. And the kingdom, while not truly wondrous, had parts that were, at times, rather remarkable. (*"What the . . . ?"* said you know who.)

She was a beautiful immigrant, with honeyed skin and almond eyes, from a land of sun and jewel-like colors, the balmy breeze fragrant with the scent of flowers and herbs that grew in abundance, the air full of tiny clanging bells from the roaming goats and of the songs the villagers sang as they walked to the glittering stream to fill the jugs they carried . . .

No. There she goes again. She was no such thing. But as she walked down the city sidewalk – with its glass shards and papers and napkins and cups blowing, its vendors selling books and incense and roasted peanuts and scarves and sunglasses and handbags and falafel, getting bumped and jostled, waving away leaflets that were pushed in her face by people, some of them actual immigrants, just trying to make a living, after all — she imagined an open, richly-colored, sun-filled land as her place of origin, from long ago. A place where she could go barefoot, gaze up at a blue sky, or walk by moonlight back to her thatched hut after an evening of song by a large bonfire in the neighboring field. Or she imagined wandering through the weekly bazaar, delighting in the spread of spices and fruits and vegetables and bolts of colorful fabric and pottery and pretty rocks and shells.

The problem with the would-be princess was that she was always mentally somewhere else, as she was well aware. On her way to her receptionist job – where she worked Monday through Friday in Midtown Manhattan on the 28th floor of an old building – if a tourist or visitor or some nervous young person applying for a job looked as if they were going to stop and ask her for directions, the words poised on her tongue were always: *Don't ask me – I'm barely here.* Instead, she would politely direct them as best she could, and then return to the imagined village stream, the bazaar, the moonlight, the deep green grasses or golden sands, depending on which geographical land she decided she was from.

One day – a Saturday before her shift began at the restaurant where she worked on weekends and Wednesday and Friday nights to have enough money for her classes that she took on Tuesday and Thursday nights, hoping to graduate in two years, studying to be teacher so that she could make some money to get a nicer apartment, help out her family, and hopefully make a difference in the lives of a student here and there – she passed a street fair.

She had to walk the seven blocks anyway, so she strolled down the avenue, taking in the booths and stalls and tables, and thinking that it was not unlike the bazaar of her imagined place of origin, except for what was sold. She looked at the displays of T-shirts and caps and fruit shakes and Belgian crepes, the Persian rugs and Peruvian sweaters and discounted bedsheet sets, the kettle corn and jewelry and assorted batteries and handmade baby clothes – and stopped.

On the table of jewelry among the trays and mirrors and boxes of beads she saw some pearls that caught her eye. Small Baroque pearls. Long strands of different lengths and different colors – pale gray and deep gray, soft pink, white, and a smaller display of bracelets strung together with elastic, easy to slip on and off. Gasp. Twenty to twenty-five dollars for the shorter necklaces – and where would she wear them anyway? But only four dollars for the bracelets – and she could wear them to work or school or even to the restaurant, a tiny glimmer of white showing below her waiter's sleeve. She purchased the bracelet and held it up, delighting in the way the sun played on the uneven shapes, bright points of lustrous lights next to shadowy curves, a hint of rainbow iridescence in each bead.

She wore the pearl bracelet that day through both shifts and admired it on her way home as she rode the subway. It made her feel rich, a thing of beauty that she could take with her everywhere. She also wore it to her receptionist job, and to class, and to the school library and bookstore, and the grocery store and laundromat, and sometimes even to bed.

Until one day, on the glass-and-trash-and-paper-strewn-sidewalk with black spots of old chewing gum, the bracelet snagged on the bag of a passerby, who didn't even notice it had caught, and the worn elastic snapped and sent the pearls scattering in all directions. Most of them tumbled into the subway grate, some rolled down into the gutter, and others popped into the traffic. For such an inexpensive trinket from a street fair, the dissolution of the bracelet filled her with unexpected sadness. She picked up the few pearls she found amid the boots and shoes and carts and little legs and big legs and put them in her pocket.

She imagined that the bracelet had broken in the bazaar of her place of origin, and that the beauty of the lustrous white pearls had caught the attention of the little barefoot girls playing among the stalls. She thought, *Why not give these girls a little pearl each?* As they gathered round her, she handed them each a white pearl. They smiled and became enriched and marveled at the tiny rainbow locked inside each bead.

"These are magical dream beads," the would-be princess explained. "You must gaze at the pearl and make a beautiful dream and lock the dream inside the pearl. Then, just before you go to sleep every night, look at the pearl and dream of your dream."

In all the minds of the little girls of the imaginary village, dreams of beauty began to swirl into being, causing their eyes to brighten and their smiles to widen. Except for one little girl with a lost look in her eye – whose life had been one long tale of sweeping and gathering firewood and cleaning the ashes and carrying water from the stream and cooking and tending the chickens and sweeping some more – who asked simply, "Why?"

"Why?" echoed the would-be princess, "why, so that you will always have something beautiful in your mind to tend to." A flicker of light went on behind the little girl's eyes, and she made a fist around the tiny pearl and carried it home and found a string to thread through the bead and wore it around her neck, tucked into her tunic where no one could see it and every night just before she went to sleep, she took out the pearl and fell in love with its soft luster and the beautiful dream inside of it that grew and grew and filled her.

When the would-be princess arrived home to the stoop of her five-floor walk-up, she saw a little girl with dull eyes sitting with her head in her hands. The princess-receptionist-waitress-student-beautiful immigrant-dreamer girl took out the pearls from her pocket and handed them to the little girl, saying, "Here. Magic pearls for a beautiful princess."

And the little girl's dull eyes turned into bright gems, reflecting the sunlight of her wondrous place of origin.

The End

It was a Rococo sky, all swirls and filigrees, excessive scrolls. Overly dramatic ornamentation that was nonetheless exquisite and lovely.

Honora read over her short story and gave that deep exhale of satisfaction when something clicks in a story. When something from inside takes shape on paper outside. She told herself it didn't matter if the story was good or not, what was important –

("*Pshaw! Don't give me that!*" said Nora. "*If you want to make it as a writer, the story better be good. If you want to pay the bills, you can't afford to be so cavalier about it.*"

Honey jolted up from her nap, and her head snapped over to Nora. "*Pshaw? I've never heard you say that! I don't think that's one of our words.*"

Nora looked away, slight abashed. "*Just trying something new.*")

Honora had noticed that over the years, Nora was becoming more experimental, more creative, while Honey was now a bit more critical. The explanation was simple. After so many years, they had rubbed off on each other.

Though Honora filled the assignments for class, it was a struggle, and the outcome was mediocre, at best. She felt scattered. Too many classes, too many writing forms? Too many unfinished pieces? Too much general confusion about life and love and jobs and money and what she even wanted out of life?

It nagged at Honora, leaving Cinderella traipsing through time all on her own. Was that poor girl still looking for a decent job and a place to live and a meaningful life? Whatever happened to her after she stole that shawl and ran away? Could the story shed some light on her own problematic trajectory? Was art imitating life? Or was it the other way around?

Honora opened her notebook to a new page to continue the forsaken tale.

"Cinderella (cont.)"

Cinderella confronted her years of guilt over stealing the beautiful, gold-threaded shawl. She scraped together her savings in hopes of being able to purchase it. She went back to the manor house and confessed what she had done to the lady of the manor. Who replied, with a flick of her hand, "That old thing? It was a gift from a great aunt, and I never much liked her or the shawl. You can keep it. I have a thousand others that I don't much care for either."

Cinderella was struck by the bored unhappiness of this fine lady with a thousand unwanted shawls. The confession helped to lift the burden of her theft. The sin was somewhat lessened, but so was the value of the shawl.

(Honey and Nora exchanged a glance.) Honora shut the notebook, uninspired.

(Honey took pity on her and put on her thinking cap. *"How about – Cinderella marries not the prince, but his younger half-brother who has been disinherited?"*

Nora gave a grunt of disbelief. *"If we're making things up, we're at least going to make sure she ends up wealthy."*

"Fair point," Honey conceded. *"How about – she meets a handsome traveler from a faraway land and –"*

Nora cut in – *"Been there, done that."*

Honey blanched – that sounded dangerously close to Honora's failing great romance. Honey quickly came up with another option. *"What about – Cinderella becomes a famous chef?"*

Nora gave a scornful sigh. *"I think not."*

"Okay, then you *come up with something."*

Nora lifted her chin and gave it a try. *"Cinderella fights against an evil emperor – or a mean queen – or something . . ."*

Honey yawned. *"Not as easy as it looks, is it?"*

Nora gave a flick of the whip in exasperation and winced when it caught her on the leg. *"Ow! That hurt."*

"You should get rid of that thing," said Honey.)

Honora wondered if this Cinderella would ever find love. She threw the notebook onto the couch, grabbed her coat, and went on a long walk.

Is this the end of Act II? Or in the five-act version, is it the end of Act III? God forbid, of Act IV? Where am I in this story of mine?

∽⤞∾

So much of Honora's relationship with him reminded her of a ride on the subway during rush hour. There she was – in a good mood for no particular reason, or engrossed in a book, or a daydream – when all of a sudden, she feels a sharp elbow or a sudden bump from a backpack or a rough shove. Infuriated at the intrusion, the rudeness, the injustice! And it hurt! Then she whips around to see who did it – only to discover that, not only was it unintentional, they weren't even aware they had done it. All that anger and getting riled up, poised for a confrontation – for nothing. Nothing was meant. It was all a misunderstanding, or even less than that. It was nothing.

∽⤞∾

Honora walked the streets of her pretty neighborhood almost every day. In the spring it was bursting with color – shooting rays of yellow forsythias, azalea bushes so thick with purple or red or coral blooms that they scarcely showed any leaves. There weren't many lilac bushes, but Honora knew where they were and would linger next to them, or stand under the branches arching over a tall fence, to breath in their fragrance.

There had been a magnificent old wisteria with massive, thick ropes of vines climbing an old sycamore, draping sweetness and pale-purple beauty overhead in the spring. It had been pure magic and every spring Honora looked forward to seeing it, raising her face to bathe in its perfume, filling herself with its beauty.

But one day, the City Parks Department destroyed the roots and truncated the vines three feet from the ground, leaving the upper part still clinging to the tree. "It's a parasite!" they argued. (*"So are you!"* hollered Nora.)

Even now, years later, when Honora passed the dead vines still twined lovingly (to her mind) around the upper tree, it felt like a blow to her heart, and she longed for the magic that was once there.

In the summer evenings, Honora took strolls and remembered the few vacations she had taken, those quaint European streets, where the elderly women had greeted her so graciously *–Bonjour, madame!* Though the dream of living in Paris had not happened, she had a poster of old Paris that she still gazed at longingly and conjured stories about.

She feared that one day, she would look at it and think: It's just a city. And then the beautiful dream that was would be gone.

⚬⚬

On her days off in the fall, Honora would rush out at the end of day, and through the bare trees, look towards the western sky to see what color and clouds it had to offer – and wonder if her future held more. Or was sky gazing to be the high point of her life?

Dream remnants. Is that all that was left?

In the winter, she wandered to the empty playground, sat on a swing, and gave herself a little push. What were all those early dreams? With a hint of a smile, she asked herself, *Remember the trapeze artist dream?*

But the smile disappeared. She couldn't imagine herself swinging on a trapeze anymore. Was it the height? The doubt that someone would catch her? Or did flying through the air no longer hold the same appeal it once did? If she was honest, she had to admit that even the back and forth of the playground swing was making her feel a little queasy.

She planted her feet to stop the rocking and sat staring at the darkening playground.

On all her walks, as she made her way back home, she looked forward to fixing a cup of tea, and opening her notebook. That was the thing about writing. She would never outgrow it. It was always there for her.

A heavy heart. She had to ask herself – were they simply dying a natural death? Had their love been doomed from the beginning?

"The Laundromat"

A snowy January day, rigid with cold. A day rimmed in stiffness and iciness and frozen hearts. In the laundromat, the ever-present contention in their minds. It's cold inside, no heat. A light despair hovers, as they toss the wet clothes into the dryer. Hands lightly touching, but without that old spark. Now they were just hands bumping.

In a spinning dryer, Honora caught a flash of soft yellow, a happy tumble, a soft patting on the dryer glass. A tablecloth? A bedspread? Pale yellow with green leaves and pink roses, and it somehow filled her with hope, renewed promise. To know that sweetness was somewhere in the world, some memory of afternoon days or spring beginnings. Or even just the actual thing itself – a cloth of pretty colors on a cold gray day, tumbling lightly in the cold.

And that is enough. Enough at least, for this day. This unlikely dryer window. This surprise of unexpected hope, a tiny connection.

They had both given all of themselves. And still, it failed. Failed? Fell apart, covered up the best parts of themselves. Yes, failed. It was she who had made the break. He would have kept trying, trying. It was becoming painful to watch him try so hard. (Honey gently touched her shoulder.) Honora nodded. "I know, I know. Not in this notebook. Or anywhere."

As she grew older, Honora relinquished dreams like ballast in order to survive, to stay afloat. As she had given up being a trapeze artist, she now gave up the dream of living abroad. She knew now that, though she might take an occasional trip, she would never be the world traveler like her uncle had been. She might polish up her Spanish or French, but she would not be the polyglot she had once dreamed of being. It was too late now to be wife and mother, part of a fairytale family of happiness. Too late for so many things. Even Cinderella was getting old, with stiff joints, and the first gray appearing in her hair.

What was that old line about sinking? Something about if I don't keep moving or trying, I will surely sink. What was the remedy? The counter? I don't remember.

NOTEBOOK 3

Today, there is snow and mist outside her corporate aerie. Honora often stayed late to work on her novel, but the end of day rarely produced any words. She stood at the window and gazed across at the Sherry Netherland building with its gargoyles and green peaked roof and tower. A soft glow came from a window high in the roof. She used to imagine a writer scribbling there at a desk, or an artist at her canvas. But her coworker had assured her it was nothing so romantic – it was most likely a generator.

Behind the stunning Art Deco building, spread the backdrop of Central Park with its lacey bare trees. Ice skaters glided round and round the rink. Patches of pure white on the fields, the ice-covered pond. Soft blue dusk. The lamplights came on and filled the park with tiny dots of gold. *I would call it beautiful*, Honora thought.

Once in a great while, Honora's jobs offered unexpected boons, such as this view from the 35th floor overlooking

Central Park. A view that changed dramatically with the weather, the seasons. A view for which she was grateful.

After fighting the grip of the corporate world for so many years, she had finally given in. It came at a cost, as does everything. But it had provided structure and some degree of security. The biggest problem was the matter of time. There was simply less of it. And the artist's life had been diminished. But what is life, she asked, if not a series of compromises. (Honey shot Nora a look of blame. *"She didn't use to think in platitudes."*)

At least she still had her notebooks, Honora thought. She no longer took classes or submitted pieces to contests and agents, but she still wrote. And perhaps one day . . .

Honora gave a parting glance at the gold and blue park, and at the writer's candlelit garret window. Then she closed her patiently waiting notebook and gave her desk a once over before leaving for the day.

If life had gone according to plan, there would have been more notebooks by now. Volume 7 or 20 – but things had gotten in the way. Love, jobs, moving, disappointments.

And yet, when Honora had written at the beginning of the new notebook: *Book the Third*, she had felt the old familiar flutter. Everything was interconnected, after all. The good the bad the ups the downs.

One job had led to another and another and another in various corporate industries. Honora became one of the millions waking, taking the train into the city, getting bumped on the crowded streets, pushing through revolving doors, and pressing elevator buttons.

The work itself remained a blur and fell under the general rubric of "helper." The jobs involved assisting with companies' charitable giving programs and special events, or supporting a boss for building projects, or helping to set up board meetings, committee meetings, summits, "new initiatives" and team building activities. Or simply doing whatever it took to make a boss's day smoother – problem solving in advance, Honora often thought of it.

And of course, there was always the base work: phones, files, faxing, copying, travel arrangements, expense reports, meetings, reservations, proofing memos/reports/letters, and general "fetching" – urgent hand deliveries, signatures needed from different floors, lunches picked up for starving bosses. And the errands on a more personal level: stamps from the post office, flowers ordered for anniversaries/weddings/funerals, a dash to the pharmacy to pick up prescriptions or an emergency pair of reading glasses, and even, a few times, help with a son's or daughter's book reports. (*"So, that degree in English finally came in handy!"* Nora said. Honey glared. *"At least those reports provided some meaning."*)

However, the unattractive aspects of the corporate world were balanced by regular paychecks, vacation pay, sick days, benefits. Honora couldn't afford to turn it down. And yet the years had passed by her silently, and more quickly than had ever seemed possible.

Initially, the permanent positions had enabled her to take more classes, to get another degree (*"Which they paid for!"* Nora reminded Honey, still arguing for the practicality of the corporate world), to better furnish her apartment, and to finally see more of the world. Irony of ironies, it was the corporate world that had made some of her dreams come true. Especially the dream of traveling. (On this point, Honey agreed. *"That alone makes it worthwhile. I guess."*)

Such sweet memories of those days of discovery. A re-bolstering of her spirit, her dreams, her essence. Nothing quite compared to exploring those wondrous cities: Istanbul. Prague. Edinburgh.

That memory of waking up in Venice: *Now then, I take map in hand and venture forth!* After recrossing the same bridge for the third time, she had ditched the map and freely wandered the enchanting city. Just like Magoo, an apparently random meandering of turning left, right, over there, what's that? But also like Magoo, safely ending up at her destination, her hotel at end of day.

Honora still fled over her lunch breaks and wandered through Central Park, or along the streets of Manhattan, and let her mind fill with story lines, impressions, and descriptions of her beloved city. She still filled her notebook.

In winter, there is solace in the bleak gray days, the bare shaking limbs of leafless trees. In the laden white-gray clouds ready to release their load of snow.

On a gray, nothing day, heavy with the weight of the week, Honora passed some workmen welding at a construction site. From across the street, she stopped to watch the tiny gold-white sparks shooting off, blue in there too, somewhere. Sudden showers of gold. Lines of stiff, quick fire, happy sparkler-like playfulness around the torch. Bright gold, luminous gas-blue, white streaks. Stars form, and a sun, in the center-of-the-universe blowtorch. A perfect world, right there in the dimness of the scaffolding.

Those little sparks of fire, primordial, eternal, the same sparks that flew off two stones of flint eons ago, the same sparks that flew in the rebirth of the sun. There, in the mundane gray of day, tiny sparks of chaos creating order. There, a little bit of man is playing God. There, a tiny beauty that both lifts and deepens the day.

Besides her one great love, her only love, there had been others who had touched upon the idea of marriage. Such a Cinderella-like ending would have been convenient in an all-problems-solved sort of way. Honey probably would have gone along with it, and made the best of things, but there was no way Nora could ever be convinced to give up her autonomy only to settle on a half-hearted life. And so they struggled on.

Jobs happened, degrees happened, the ups and downs happened, the day to day became the year to year, and Honora filled her notebook. And (thanks to Honey's persistence) she continued to enrich her days with music and books and flowers and tea and all things lovely and beautiful. And yet.

Sometimes the disappointments and the weight of the outside world, human nature, history repeating itself over and over, pulled her down. It sometimes became hard to call up her earlier, optimistic, youthful self.

∾⚬∾

"In my search for the sweetness of life, I discovered the bracing stringency of bitterness. And found that its sure-footedness served me rather well." – HG

(Nora caught Honey's eye and mouthed – *sour grapes*? Honey shrugged and gave a sad nod.)

∾⚬∾

The news, the news. It was all so horrible. Honora kept telling herself to stop watching it, and yet it was hard to escape. It was everywhere and it was all so depressing. The shock of realizing that the worst parts of human nature were still thriving. The myth (or had it been simply hope?) was dispelled. The horrors of humankind – of medieval times, of WWII, and even more recently – were not aberrations of history. They were history. Soulless cruelty was always there, just waiting to pounce on the unsuspecting world, with claws out, fangs positioned, and millennia of honed experience at its beck and call. The terrifying notion that "it" had been let loose. Evil was exploding, spreading, taking over once again. What chance did sweet little goodness and kindness have against such a powerful and ancient force?

The sky today . . .

(Both Nora and Honey scanned the sky but didn't find a single thing of interest.)

"The Creature FineMind"

I lay in darkness for thousands of years at a time. Surfacing after eons, then sliding back down into the black velvet. Deep beneath roiling oceans, seismic earth. I lay still, wrapped in

Soft Time. As Hard Time worked on the elements and mind, allowing for development, I lay in deep being.

Four, five hundred years, tendrils of thought cast up to observe, assess, finding the same cramped minds of humans, warring, greedy, cruel. In specks of time only, an occasional spark of fine-mind catching fire and sometimes spreading, to raise dull animal struggle into light. How they crumbled to their knees and gasped in awe, at knowing what could be.

I lay in darkness, rising only when the geyser of thought coalesced and pushed me up. Then. Then I rose. Shouldering chunks of time and earth away from me, surfacing through shining light and the roll of years of days and nights. I rose, stretching and exuberating in wakefulness. I rose to fan the fire of thought, of fine-mind creating beauty and meaning, so that it could form the next level, and take itself, and me, to the end beginning. I rose to fan the fire – and to extinguish the mean, the cramped, the dull.

Then. When mean-mind numbers grew again, I withdrew. Sinking once more into the layers of darkness and sleep.

Don't let them fool you about rock bottom. There's something about it that comes almost as a comfort. The horror and fear of slipping and sliding, the dreadful descent into chaos, where the glimmers of hope become fainter and fainter – all that ceases.

Rock bottom is still and quiet, cool and dark. Pitch black. It's cold and lonely, for you can only go there by yourself. But there is comfort in knowing that the falling has stopped. For the moment, nothing else is expected of you. It's not that things can't get worse – they always can. But the difference is that at rock bottom, it no longer matters.

Honora sat at her writing desk, remembering conversations with her grandmother who had assured her that although she loved life and had enjoyed a full one, the difficulties and limitations of age prepare you for moving on to whatever is next.

Honora jotted down a few lines, sat back and read them. Then she poked around for that tattered folder labeled "Bad Poetry" – and remembered that she had tossed it away years ago.

"One by one the pleasures leave, to ease the exit, it seems.

Joys of the body, delights of the mind. The last to go are dreams." - HG

(*"Oh no you don't!"* cried Nora. *"Stop with the negativity! Look – you've made Honey cry."*)

All right, all right. Honora folded the scrap of paper into an airplane and sent it flying into the trash can.

It came as a disappointment when she finally revisited Caffe Reggio. She had half-expected to step into her old self, for her old dream to be waiting for her as she took a seat at the same round table she had sat at so many years ago (only this time she kept bumping her knees against the carved table legs.) Why did it all feel so different? She looked at the walls – had they been painted a different color? Had they rearranged the place? Was it smaller? The wait staff, the customers were younger, less attentive, engrossed in devices. Where was the buzz of creativity? Where was the cohesion of music, paintings, notebooks, and dreams?

A few more jobs, a few more years. From Honora's latest office desk, the sky towards the Hudson River was slowly being blocked out by construction. New buildings going up, all over the place. And of course, bigger was always better. The old city was disappearing. She felt the same sense of loss when she waited on the platform in Queens and viewed the city from afar. She sighed. All the blue sky (that now gave her such pleasure) was disappearing, patch by patch. Slowly, it was being obliterated by new tall buildings.

Honora gazed out at the skyline and thought – The city has changed. It's not the same.

The city looked back and said – I could say the same for you.

"The Gentleman Grim"

You'd think he would have updated his appearance.

He was not one to ignore, try as you might – sitting there in his long dark garb, staff in his hand. I had long ago determined to ignore his presence and go about my business with life. I saw him at the end of the path, always sitting on a large boulder that functioned as a sort of seat for him, staring straight ahead. Grim and taciturn – no fun at all.

Oftentimes, when I looked his way, I would find him fixed on me – a bit unnerving, let me tell you. But, like the gentleman he was, he would always politely turn away. Yes, yes, I would think – I see you there. No need to remind me. Just go about your business and let me go about mine.

We lived in uneasy coexistence – with his hooded face turned towards me at the death of my father, then my mother. At the death of my friend. He began to feel more familiar.

As I made my way along life's path, and came nearer the figure, I saw that the staff was an actual scythe, a reaper's scythe, and I was about to laugh out loud at the absurdity. But then I saw that it was very old, polished with age, and had been with him for long years – a staff that had helped to support him through Time. He was probably attached to it, sentimental value. I certainly didn't begrudge him his aid. Goodness, we all need a cane, or walking stick, or a helping hand on our long journey. So he used a scythe, so what? We're all entitled to our choices. The closer I got to him, the more I found myself allied with him. It was only from a distance that he had appeared so formidable, so grim, so – unappealing.

After the twists, and stumbles, and uphill struggles along the path, I grew weary. The gentleman Grim moved aside and offered to share his seat with me, which I quite appreciated. After I rested, we left together on our path. He kindly allowed me to place a hand on his old worn scythe, for support. I must say, I found it most welcome.

"The Ice Cream Truck"

It is both delightful and maddening, the music that comes from the ice cream truck in the summers. Some children's la la-la-la song that plays loudly as the truck wends its way through the neighborhood. It always comes at the same time, around sunset. You can hear its approach several blocks away. The sound is deafening when it idles in front of the house. Sometimes I close the windows, blocking out the sound and the fumes. But isn't ice cream one of the happy things about summer? Isn't that song meant to evoke the joys of childhood and summertime pleasures? Sometimes no one comes and the ice cream man drives away. At other times he has a line of people waiting – both adults and children. It is a happy thing.

The other day, the truck stopped outside one of the row houses in the late summer evening. A young mother and her little girl came to the truck. The mother pointed to one of the pictures of ice cream cones painted on the side. The little girl had long braids and moved her hands to the tune of the playful music. The mother paid and took the ice cream from the man. Smiling, she leaned over to her little girl and said something. The little girl gave her a quick kiss, and then took the ice cream. A happy thing.

From an upstairs window, a childless woman looked on in the dark and wept bitter tears for what might have been. Then the ice cream truck drove away, its happy music fading in the distance.

(A loud crack of the whip, Nora's face sharp and challenging. *"You're not going to get all maudlin and self-pitying at this stage of the game, are you?"*)

Honora tried not to cry. "It's just that I still – seeing him with that beautiful little boy on his shoulders took me by surprise. I could barely breathe. I can't help thinking – that could have been our . . . my little –"

(Nora wagged her finger. *"Ah ah ah – No regrets. That was your motto."*

"You knew he had married," Honey gently offered.

Nora put her hands on her hips. *"It's been ten years! And remember, you're the one who turned him down! You wanted –"*)

Honora raised her voice and snapped, "You don't have to remind me! You know, sometimes I don't like you very much!"

(Nora jerked her head back, hurt – and surprised – that was something *she* would say. She had always known that sweet, gentle Honey was the favored one. Nora glanced over at Honey, curled up in her long velvet skirt looking tragic. Nora folded her arms across her chest and began to sulk – she was never appreciated.)

After hours of walking, deep in thought, Honora entered the neighborhood park and sat on a bench. She opened her notebook. Raised her eyes to the trees. Lifted her pen. But the words wouldn't come.

She watched the children play, as always, loving the sound of their exuberance, their laughter, the necessity to run. Why walk when you can run? Such joy, such energy, such promise.

She and her siblings had been just like that – so full of happiness. Family was such a beautiful thing. Perhaps one of the most beautiful things of all.

She took in a deep breath, blew it out, and looked around.

(Honey sat with shoulders slumped, still looking tragic – though perhaps now with a hint of the melodramatic.)

"What. What is it?" Honora asked her with a bit of impatience. "What are you thinking about?"

(Honey lifted her face and sighed. *"Remember old Georgie? At the funeral. He was such a figure of grief. I can't get it out of my mind. He stood there, leaning on his cane, silent tears running down his creased cheeks. Maybe it's true that we become more emotional with age."* She wiped away a tear. *"And I know how you feel. Seeing 'him', with his beautiful little son on his shoulders – well, that kind of broke my heart. Life – life can be so, so . . .")*

Honora glanced over at Nora, hoping to rely on her strength. But even she was down in the dumps. Usually ramrod straight and up for a challenge, Nora now sat slouched, staring out at nothing, using her thumb to chip away at her red nail polish.

Honora closed her notebook and took a deep breath. Then she lightly nudged them. "Come on. Let's go on a walk. Find some clouds."

Honey nodded but didn't say anything. Another nudge got Nora to her feet.

Honora tried to inject some enthusiasm into her voice. "We'll stop by a café. Get a cappuccino and jot down some ideas for – I don't know, something."

After the café, they strolled home. Once the caffeine had kicked in, and they were somewhat revived, the three of them agreed: *This won't do. All these weary and dark meanderings of mind. Life is too short for that.*

Honora had to admit that she had lost touch with her old self, her writing self, her communication with life. And without that she was untethered, lost, lonely, not happy.

"I must get back to that earlier, happier of way of being," said Honora. "And you two are going to help me! Strength in numbers."

(They nodded in encouragement. Honey suggested, *"Another fairytale? A poetry class? A new skirt?"* Nora had other ideas. *"Let's plan the next journey. You've always wanted to see Patagonia. Or perhaps the Amalfi Coast?"*)

Honora gave Nora (who was only happy when she was busy) the task of finding another class and possible travel destinations. Nora was soon gleefully tapping away at the computer, making lists.

And she sent Honey on a mission to buy flowers from the vendor on the corner. "Something bright and cheerful! And get a bottle of champagne while you're at it. We're going to celebrate!"

The sky tonight holds magic. Through the window, over the slate rooftops, a full moon rises through the leafy tree branches and illuminates the clouds in gold.

∽

For the most part, Honora's new-found resolution had stuck and she tried to fuel it with all her old loves. She used to dream of one day having a beautiful old piano, like the one her friends in Seattle had – vintage oak, with carved wood and ivory keys, the baby grand positioned in the spacious living room overlooking Puget Sound.

That dream had recently morphed into purchasing an actual piano ("*keyboard*," corrected Nora in a disparaging tone, "*with volume control.*" Honey defended the choice. *"It's better than nothing."*)

Honora had missed having a piano all these years, and now the little computerized *keyboard* stood wedged between the kitchen table and the back of the couch. She had forgotten so much, and her fingers felt stiff. Her attempts at trills were laughable. If only she had kept up with it. The pieces she once played with ease were now a struggle.

Nevertheless, some nights, she poured a glass of wine or champagne, turned on only the leaf lamp so that the room was softly lit, and sat at the piano (yes, yes, the *keyboard*.) She would gaze out the window at the dark sky, the little lights of the homes and the taller apartment buildings behind them and enter the magic of the night world. And feel her old self coming alive.

What would it sound like, she wondered, that golden, delicate moon rising through the night sky, in and out of those thin clouds? She found a small, high chord on the piano. And repeated it, adding two short single notes. And again. That was it! There it was! The sound of moonlight.

From that moment, Honora played her own music, stunned to realize that the songs had been there all along in the keys. It was easier and more enjoyable than trying to read music at this stage.

She found many songs over the years, naming them by the images they evoked: *Carcassonne, Moonlight, Black-key Lullaby, the Rain, the Dark-gabled House, Springtime.* They all had stories that went with them, which she would one day write out in her notebooks.

⤬

After one such mesmerizing night, Honora felt grateful for all that she had. For the love and the dreams and the joy that had filled her life. (*I think that's the champagne speaking,*" said Nora. Honey raised her glass and took another sip. "*So what if it is? Cheers, Nora.*")

Honora felt a story emerging, craving expression. She became overwhelmed by nostalgia for her earlier self – which was now, she understood, a part of her older self. She wanted to write about the things she loved, still loved. Love for the world, for travel, for books and learning, for connecting with others, for dreams. She would have to locate the corresponding song in the piano keys. For now, she would express it in her notebook. And for old times' sake, she would make it a fairytale.

The Cobbler's Woeful Globe

One day, hundreds of years ago, an old cobbler made a pair of splendid boots for a passing traveler. The traveling man was so pleased with the new boots that he gave the cobbler one of his prized possessions, a newly made globe, and then went on his way.

The cobbler took the globe home, and sat it next to him near the fire. Slowly, he spun it around in his old, gnarly hands, studying it carefully. And when he saw the vast oceans and the new lands and islands, tears filled his eyes, and he wept. He wept for the wideness of the world, and his own small lot in it. He was a cobbler who had never left his seaside village. And now he was old.

Turning the globe round in his hands and weeping all the while, he heard a metal chinking sound as his tears hit the ground. Looking down by his feet he saw that his tears had turned into coins. But it didn't make him any happier – in fact, he wept all the more.

At first, the villagers were astounded by the transforming tears, and were happy to receive a few stray coins. But the coins of sadness never brought happiness to anyone. So as time passed by, they simply helped the old cobbler to gather them.

The cobbler built small coffers to store the coins in, and the rooms of his cottage soon became stacked with wooden chests. For every time he saw the globe he wept – and he saw it first thing in the morning and last thing at night. He gave the globe a loving pat before climbing into bed, murmuring softly as he wept, "Oh, the world, the world."

This went on for months, and then years, and he had to make a special storehouse just for the coffers. He became miserably wealthy. He thought it was one of life's cruel jokes that all his years he longed to be rich, and now that he finally was, he didn't care. All he wanted was the world.

The old cobbler often hobbled down to the shore and gazed out at the distant horizon, dreaming of faraway places. And though there was no one to man it, and he was too old, he had a three-masted ship built. Seeing his beautiful ship on the water slowed down his tears and filled him with hope.

One sunny morning, the cobbler was visited by a scruffy young lad from a neighboring village. He had heard about the cobbler and his globe, the coins, and the three-masted ship. The cobbler invited him in and showed him the globe. The scruffy lad leaned over and slowly turned the globe around, gazing at it with great curious eyes.

"What's on your mind, lad?" the old cobbler asked.

The youth looked up, swallowed hard, and spoke the words that filled his heart. He clasped his hands in front of him and stood tall. "I want to see the world! I want to be an explorer. I want to sail the seven seas!"

The old man sat on the wooden bench next to the globe, his crooked hands resting on his cane. He looked at the lad compassionately and sighed. "That's a grand idea, and a fine one, too. But you need many things for that, least of all a ship and coins." He gave the lad a meaningful nod. "You have to be able to read and to write, and to sail by the stars. You must know languages, the laws of nature, and the ways of the world."

The scruffy lad cast his eyes down in shame. He was, as everyone knew, Tom Doolen – the worst student the twelve coastal villages had ever known. He couldn't read, he could barely write his name, he flunked mathematics horribly, and had slept through astronomy. His grades were so bad that everyone thought he was stupid. Instead of going to his classes, he headed off into the woods in search of adventure. Tom just couldn't see the point of letters and numbers, equations and facts. Until now.

The old man understood the lad's plight and wanted to encourage him. "I, too, have a burning desire for the world, but I am too old now. I can barely hobble down to the shore and back," he said, rubbing his rheumy knees. "At least you are young. You still have a chance."

The lad looked up hopefully. "Give me one year, and see what I may learn."

"One year, then. And good luck," said the cobbler.

From that day forward, Tom Doolen was a different lad. He seemed to turn into a young man overnight. Suddenly mathematics and science were easy for him. He read morning, noon, and night. He studied several languages, and even reveled in poetry, drama, and philosophy. A door had opened inside of him, and his world was expanding day by day.

One year passed. With a large trunk on his back, and no longer scruffy, Tom walked to the cobbler's village. First, he strode down to the shore and gazed longingly at the beautiful ship. Then he went to the old cobbler's home and noticed yet another storehouse built for the coins. Tom felt sorry for the cobbler and hoped he could bring some happiness to the old man's life.

The door to the cobbler's home stood open. Tom heard the *chink, chink* of falling tears, and followed the sound out to the garden. The old man sat on a bench with his globe next to him, and with a stick in his hand, he was drawing the world in the dirt. Shapes of new lands and wide oceans spread before him. *Chink, chink*, fell his tears.

The cobbler looked up and saw before him a young man with bright, determined eyes. He didn't recognize Tom at first, so greatly had the lad changed. Then the old man dried his tears, pushed himself up, and embraced Tom.

"My kindred spirit," he said, "has one year gone by? I hadn't noticed. I must be getting old."

"I have a surprise for you," Tom said, smiling all the while. He helped the cobbler back to his bench and set the trunk before him. When he opened the lid, the cobbler's eyes widened in astonishment. The trunk was filled with volumes of books, maps, and grids. There was a magnificent astrolabe and a marvelous compass. Charts of the stars and of the islands of the world. Tom set about explaining the function of each item. He read from the books, talked of the stars, and composed a poem on the spot. The old man was enchanted.

The cobbler then closed the trunk and put a shaky hand on Tom's shoulder. "Yes, the time has come. Go and explore the world and write to me everything that you see. In that way, I will be fulfilled. Take the ship and what coins you need."

Tom manned the ship, and stocked it well, and then set off with the tide.

The old cobbler never wept again from that day forward. He received letters and maps regularly. Captain Tom had a special surprise for him, too. During his journeys and explorations, he had taught himself to draw and paint, so that the cobbler could see the faraway lands, as well as read about them. All around his home hung paintings of exotic places that Tom had seen: desert oases and camel caravans, pointed pagodas and towering temples, labyrinthine bazaars and tropical islands. The old cobbler's world was at last a very large one.

The cobbler helped other young men to get their start on the seas, and several scholar-captains followed Tom. After many ships, and many voyages of many years, the coin supply finally dwindled down. But the old man was always well provided for by Captain Tom, who was the most well-loved and respected captain on the seas. To every port he brought books and helped the children to read and paint. He told them about the old cobbler, and how he had made it possible for him, Tom, to sail the seven seas and explore the world. So not only did the cobbler receive letters and drawings from Tom, but from children all over the world.

Every evening, the old cobbler sat in his garden with letters on his lap waiting to be read. And looking at his globe he would say with delight, "Ah, the world, the world."

The End

Honora flipped through her notebooks and questioned her life. She had come to the city chasing a dream and had pursued many paths. But had something happened, or had nothing happened? She sighed. Life happened, she decided, and that was what she had been after. She jotted down a postscript that she would one day add to the last of her notebooks:

> "I've smoothed out my crumpled stories and frowned one final time at my paltry attempts to tell the world how much I love it. Here they are. My notebooks. Filled with my words." – HG

In the meantime, she would be busy filling more of them. London awaited, as did Paris, and that hotel in Norway, was it? Where you went to sleep gazing at the northern lights from the skylights above your bed. She could hardy imagine such a wonder. Cairo, the Valley of the Kings, Marrakesh, oases. Perhaps she would begin a travel journal. So many places to see. All those exotic far-off lands, oceans away. *The world, the world . . .*

Blossom time. The spring was cold, with occasional snow. Then a few warm days came and the pear trees along the street burst into bloom. Honora waited all year for the month with the fluttering white blossoms, lovely against the old brick, the gray slate roofs, the softer gray of the sky. The temperature had dropped again, and she hoped the cold would keep the blossoms on the trees a little longer. But already she saw a bit of green – the leaves were beginning to show. Soon, the rains would loosen the blossoms, whisking them into the air. And she would have to wait another year for April blossoms.

In the early morning, the sounds from the train yard have a greater presence. Especially when the air is heavy with moisture, as it is today, giving the sound more to hold onto. The plaintive train whistle sounds low, not the blast of a whistle upon arrival, but a low, sustained sound that hovers in the air. A low rumble follows the train along the tracks. It is a sound that has always haunted Honora – in a good way. A secret message, reminding her that time is passing, and the dream is moving ahead, with or without her, passing through the great beauties and wonders of the world.

Honora's joints hurt in the morning. How did this happen? When did this happen? Feet, knees, hips – stiff. Walk it off. Keep going, so that you *can* keep going.

Honora had made peace with the corporate world. She no longer added "prison bars" around the words. (*"Though she still thought it,"* Honey pointed out.)

In some ways the permanent jobs had made life easier – less stress about money, those vacations, a savings account of sorts for down the road. She was even eying a small, one-family house to buy, with a private little garden.

Yes, some things were easier, but in other ways, she missed the artist's life that she had once set out to – "OH SHUT UP!!" Honora barked, startling both Nora and Honey. "Stop complaining and do something about it!!"

(Honey whispered to Nora – *"Aren't* we *supposed to say those things?"*

Nora blinked in confusion. *"It's like she's become us! She's even using my exclamation points!"*)

Natasha

It happened on the day of the confused snow. Iris dressed for another day of work, went to the kitchen, and made herself a cup of tea. As she parted the kitchen curtains, she took in a tiny gasp of surprise at the white blossoms drifting past the treetops – and then realized that they were snowflakes.

How could I have been so mistaken?

True, it had been unusually mild the day before, but the mounds of dirty snow on the sidewalks below confirmed that blossom-time was still far away. Winter claimed firm ownership over her and the sky and the day.

Iris took a sip of tea and looked out at the snowflakes. Even though she was now in her fifties, she usually took a childlike delight in snowfall, but the snow outside the window disturbed her somehow. It wasn't behaving like snow. It was blossom-sized and sparse, and blowing in every direction but down. It floated sideways and up and around, as if too light to succumb to gravity – exactly the way a brisk April breeze blew blossoms from the pear trees that lined her street.

Above the slate roofs across the way, the heavy sky cracked and shifted with dark, seismic clouds. The sun shone brokenly in unexpected starts, briefly illuminating the blossom-snow – and then retreated behind the commanding winter gray. A blast of wind scattered old leaves across the street and bounced a paper cup along the sidewalk, making tiny, hollow coughing sounds as it tumbled away.

It was cold. Everything about the day was cold. Winter fierce. Steely gray.

Why should snowflakes so disturb me? Was it the mixture of spring with winter? Do I once again feel fooled by life?

Iris took in a deep, two-layered yawn and lifted her teacup for another sip. A child's cry rose from the sidewalk. She cast her eyes down – a sweet family. The father holding the hand of a little girl, the mother pushing a stroller. When the infant cried, both parents leaned over the stroller and adjusted the blanket. The father swept up the little girl into his arms, causing her to laugh. They continued down the sidewalk, perhaps to daycare, perhaps to grandmother's.

Iris's gaze was pulled up to the sky again by a sudden wash of sunlight over the dark day, and those persistent blossom-snowflakes.

Give me all snow or all blossoms, but don't combine the two. It's too unsettling. I must force budding spring back inside, store the bulbs of scented color in the dark cupboard, pull on my boots.

She flexed her stiff fingers. *Dare I once again grasp at spring?*

No. I must remain in the hold of winter, the cold of winter, the bundling up, dark days at 5:00.

A gust of wind whisked tattered leaves from autumn up to the second floor and scattered the blossom-snowflakes, while bright shafts of sunlight pierced the gray – as if all the seasons were compressed, as if life were rushing her.

An hour later, hurrying to her job in the city, Iris walked along the sidewalk that bordered the park. She glanced at her watch now and then, in between observing the delicate snowflakes and the slants of sunlight gaining against the gray.

I really must leave my humdrum job – copy this, file these, schedule this, cancel that, a car at 6:00. I must do something else. Life passes by too quickly.

Through the bare trees she spotted a sudden patch of crystalline blue sky beginning to stake its claim. Finally, something solid to hold on to, connect to. Then, at that very moment, WHAM! – she banged her head against someone else's thought bubble and ran smack into a dark-eyed, nineteenth-century Russian character, primping in her boudoir!

Iris halted in amazement – and some degree of indignation – that this person, this idea, this Natasha, was it? had so casually waltzed into her mind.

Iris immediately understood that Natasha was a character long ago conceived but never developed, never completed. Someone had conjured her up nearly a century ago and then forgot about her. And Natasha had lingered in the ethersphere, just waiting, waiting for her story to continue.

Along with the image of Natasha, came the origins of both her and her creator, though it was all a bit fuzzy. As far as Iris could make out, Natasha had been created by Sabine, a Parisian seamstress in the 1920s.

Once a month, Sabine had slipped on her best dress, a pretty pink floral with black lace around the neck, and selected a brooch or a spray of flowers picked from her window box, grabbed her notebook, and then strolled to a certain café on *La Rue Russe*.

There, she took a seat by the window, ordered a carafe of wine, and indulged in an evening of beauty. She penned descriptions of sunset fields, leaf-strewn streets, and strands of beach. She wrote about changelings and orphans who made something of their lives, and seamstresses who, through sheer force of will, rose to become sought-out designers.

And she wrote about the beautiful Natasha, living in 1870's Russia.

But Sabine had gotten stuck. She never quite knew what to do with Natasha. The details piled up of Natasha's boudoir, her clothing and jewelry, the view from her window. Yet Natasha's story failed to develop, and so the character remained in her room.

Sabine tried out different scenarios: Natasha as the countess who discovers the talented seamstress and makes her famous. Natasha running away from her repressive family and settling in Gdansk, where she becomes a trapeze artist. Natasha falling in love with a dashing explorer and sailing with him to the South China Sea. Or did she run away with the gypsies?

Nothing seemed to work. Sabine had made Natasha too fine, too beautiful, too willful for her creator to imagine what happened next.

Of course, it was possible that Natasha's genesis began earlier. Perhaps Sabine had bumped into someone else's idea of Natasha, so that Sabine never quite understood her true nature.

At any rate, the beautiful Russian character remained unfinished, languishing in her boudoir, bored, pampered, dreaming of the wider world outside her window in snowy Saint Petersburg.

That is, until Iris bumped into her.

Oh, please! thought Iris. She didn't have time for this. She was busy sorting out her own life and didn't need someone else's plot to figure out.

And yet the more she resisted Natasha and Sabine, the more firmly they took root.

Iris sympathized with Sabine, for the burden she carried of another's fate. She imagined Sabine sitting in her cold, candlelit garret, sewing the lace-trimmed chemises and petticoats of fine ladies, and suddenly having an insight into Natasha. She would set her sewing down and add to her notes – then shake her head and pick up her sewing again.

Or perhaps Sabine wandered through a snowy Père Lachaise, her hands plunged in the pockets of her sea-green coat, as she tried to coax out the story of Natasha, pausing in front of the tomb of Molière or Balzac, in hope of inspiration.

Or maybe she sat at her table in the café, overhearing bits of conversation about The Divine Sarah or Isadora and wondered if Natasha's destiny lay with the stage.

At each incipient possibility, Natasha would quickly rise to her feet, her dark eyes sparkling in excitement as vague visions took shape in her mind – then, as Sabine nixed the ideas, Natasha would drop back onto her velvet chaise longue, or gaze out the window and sigh.

It was true that Natasha was somewhat spoiled, and her pleasures were small and indulgent. She spent her time in idle pursuits: choosing between Parisian brocades and silks to be fashioned into gowns, cutting marbled paper into pretty shapes, improving her needlepoint, and trying her maid's patience with new ways to style her hair or tie her sash.

But Iris could see that there was more to the girl – Natasha was just waiting to blossom.

She took a closer look at Sabine's Natasha. There she was, idly fluffing the bunched rosettes of pale pinks and greens on her lap cover. Natasha smoothed the glossy brown tresses draped over her shoulder and adjusted the jeweled combs, as she waited for her maid to return with her morning cocoa. She rose impatiently and stood in front of the gilded mirror, primping and pouting and trying different expressions for *le bal* for which she was forever preparing. She was outraged that *maman* insisted she wear the dull dove-gray dress to *le bal* tonight rather than the emerald gown that so beguilingly set off her eyes and hair.

As Iris watched Natasha, she realized that the girl was on the brink of womanhood. The way Natasha's hands smoothed her robe over her hips suggested awareness – delight, even – in her curves, and Iris well understood the concerns of poor *maman*. One moment of unchaperoned freedom and this girl would indeed run off with the circus or into the arms of a dashing adventurer.

And yet, thought Iris, how sad for Natasha to be trapped in eternal youth, her potential never known. She watched Natasha saunter to the window, rub away the frost flowers, and gaze at the people on the street below. Natasha wondered where they were all going, everyone in a hurry. Their cheeks red from the cold, their breath making wisps of smoke as they talked and laughed.

Natasha longed to follow them, converse with them, discover what the world was all about. She touched her pale, warm cheek and imagined it crimson with cold. She blew out a puff of air and imagined it turning into smoke. She wanted to run like the children on the street below. Gallop like the soldiers on their fine chestnut horses. Stroll through the park in the springtime, lace parasol in hand, blossoms swirling all around her. She wanted to see how her own uniqueness would play out in the world, to be tried and tested, to be shocked or delighted or dazzled by her choices and decisions. *Oh life*, she would dream. *Oh, life*.

Iris resolved that, though she may not know where the story would lead, she would at least get Natasha out the door and into the world. Let her dance at the ball and experience the dream of romance. Let her know that first thrilling glance across a crowded room that would set her heart fluttering, the first press of warm lips against her hand. Let her breathe the cold air of winter, the scented air of spring. Let her come to know the dreams of future-heavy youth, so beautiful and brief.

These were the thoughts that filled Iris's mind throughout the snow-filled day as she copied and filed and scheduled and canceled and called for a car at 6:00 – along with the image of herself at a café window.

For she knew that after work, she would walk to the little French café she sometimes passed, with the pale green exterior and hammered tin ceiling, and she would take a seat by the window. Then, Sabine-like, she would order a glass of wine and continue the story of Natasha.

And on her way home, she would walk through the swirl of snow-blossoms and inhale their springtime fragrance.

The End

The years passed and Honora kept writing and walking and looking at the sky and making plans. And dreaming. She watched the children of her nieces and nephews turn into fine young adults and was thrilled when they visited her in her little house with the garden and fireplace. They kept her in touch with the newer, younger world that was changing so rapidly.

Though her mother's world had always seemed so quaint and old-fashioned, she and her sisters recently agreed that they could relate more to their mother's world and her generation than to their children's world with its ever-changing technology. All young people were glued to devices nowadays. Everything was digital, virtual, e-everything. She could hardly keep up and was often dismayed.

When Honora rode the subway these days, she was perpetually amazed that everyone was on their phones now. Including her. When did this all happen? she wondered. I was there. Was I not paying attention? Or did it just happen a little bit at a time? One day there was Pac-Man, and the next . . . The old world was slowly vanishing. Gone were the old forms that had been around for centuries. Gone were the once ubiquitous newspapers, magazines, and books.

Honora sat in her garden. It wasn't the walled garden with a fountain that she had once dreamed of, but it was a garden nonetheless. Small, pretty. She gazed out lovingly at the climbing vines, the potted flowers, everything still glistening from the morning rain.

A little frog hopped along the puddle. "Hello, fellow creature! Where did you come from?" She leaned forward and smiled at the frog. "Don't expect a kiss from me at my age. I'm long past that fairytale stuff." (*"That will be the day!"* Nora couldn't resist interjecting.)

"Did you say something, Auntie?" Her great-niece, who was visiting for two weeks, was stretched out on a deck chair, studying.

Young, smooth-skinned, shiny hair – beautiful. All the young people were so beautiful, and they didn't have a clue. *Youth is wasted on the young.* Honora frowned as she tried to place the quote. "Who said that?"

"Talking to yourself again?" asked her niece.

"Yes, I am!" Honora replied a bit peevishly. "I'm a good listener. And you're going to get a stiff neck staring at that thing all the time."

Her niece looked around. "Oh, my phone? I'm studying my lines."

Honora observed her twenty-something niece and carried on the internal conversation to which she was such an attentive listener. *Lines. An actor? Let's see how that works out for you.*

And yet, Honora would support her and cheer her on and do what she could for her. After all, wasn't it the pursuit of the artist's path that had brought her the most joy over the course of her life?

Honora had taken up painting somewhere along the way. She now looked at the flowers she was depicting in watercolors and wondered if anyone but she would know that they were foxgloves leaning against a birdbath with two splashing birds. She put her head back an inch and studied the composition. Probably not, she decided.

Her niece looked over and admired the painting. Then she held up the digital script. "I'm going to perform a contemporary piece about a tale of transformation. It's about a young woman who . . ."

Good God! thought Honora. *She sounds just like me. Should I be concerned?* "Sounds marvelous!"

"So you'll come and watch my performance?"

"I wouldn't miss it for the world." *Ah, the fictitious life. Nothing quite compares.*

∽

"Cinderella (still cont.)"

The theme of the Cinderella story stubbornly followed Honora throughout her life: from the shy girl in grade school choosing words to the jump rope song, to identification with the 1960's television musical, to a high school Cinderella drama in which she was relegated to an extreme peripheral role, to her college class discussions of the story's cultural significance, to her own version of what happened to the hard-working, fiercely independent, sooty princess.

Inspired by her great-niece, Honora opened her note-book, determined to continue the story of youth and beauty and transformation.

However, just as she was about to indulge in the tale, she was rudely interrupted by the rebuke that came in strident, three-fold unison from Nora, Honey, and even herself:

Face it, Honora! It's too late to be Cinderella!!

She sat back. Her heart sank. She knew it to be true. Youth, beauty, first love, romance . . . gone, forever gone.

The possibilities of youth, that breathtaking moment of new beginnings, peak moments of physical beauty, uncreaky knees, gone, gone, gone.

All three of them slumped in their chairs, shoulders weighted down by defeat, disappointment, and despair – not to mention a bit of arthritis.

Then, just as the door to dejection began to open, Honora's lifelong practice of making the best of things came to her rescue. She sat up spine straight in her chair, and her index finger shot up.

"But I can still be the Fairy Godmother!"

(Honey's eyes brightened. *"I love her! She was beautiful and magical and her dress shimmered in the moonlight!"* Nora jumped to her feet, ready for action. *"And powerful! She made things happen and was completely independent! My kind of character!"*)

Honora agreed. "And she had way more fun. She controlled the magic, transforming the ordinary into the extraordinary, hanging out with mice footmen and fashioning pumpkin carriages. If it wasn't for her, Cinderella would have remained a scullery maid."

(*"And the mice would never have worn those elegant silk breeches and jackets,"* said Honey. *"I bet they talked about it for years!"*)

Honora imagined two old mice reminiscing: "Remember that time we were out nibbling at pumpkins in the garden and that fairy godmother appeared? What a night that was!" The story probably got passed down to generations of young mice.

And just like that, ten years seemed to drop from Honora. She felt lighter, happier, more powerful. "I should have thought of her years ago. She's a far more interesting character. Nora? Why are you so quiet?"

(A light shrug. *"Cinderella's been with us for so long. I think we should at least finish her story."*)

Honora gave a soft chuckle. "So, you're a sentimentalist after all. Well, of course we'll finish her story. Besides, there are still a few pages left to fill in this notebook. And then we'll get busy being the Fairy Godmother – granting wishes and living in a world of spectacular wonder."

Honora imagined traveling to Italy to visit the great-niece who had settled there. She could help her set up the new nursery.

Or offer to babysit so that her nephew and his wife could take one of those backpacking trips they so loved.

Or maybe she would treat her overworked, corporate-entrenched niece to a weekend in London – she was just saying the other day that she needed a change.

Honora smiled at the years to come. *Oh, this Fairy Godmother stuff might just be the most fun I've ever had!*

Perhaps, thought Honora, she might even go back to reading to the children and encouraging them in their dreams.

Her mind was firing, leaping about as it hadn't in a long time. She was bursting with generosity and the desire to grant dreams, encourage wishes, help young people, cheer them on!

She took up her notebook once again. "Now, where was I? Time to wrap this story up." She flipped through the notebook searching for the last entry on Cinderella. (Nora looked over her shoulder. *"I think you left her searching for yet another job."*)

"Ha! We can do better than that!"

"Cinderella (cont. to end)"

> Having decided to be more like the Fairy Godmother (art imitating life – or could they even be separated at this point?), Cinderella became known as the Gift-Giver, the Sweet Auntie, the Dream-Maker, trying her hardest to make lives better, happier, more magical.

One day, in the spirit of generosity, she even gave away her beloved shawl to a woman who ardently admired it. Cinderella arranged it around the woman's shoulder, tying it loosely in front. *Ah, it's so freeing not to need. It's so much better to give.* However, her eyes grew misty as she saw it walking away from her.

Then, not ten minutes later, she was appalled to discover that the woman had wadded it up and tossed it along the road, not really needing or wanting it. Cinderella ran and gathered it from the dusty earth, shaking the dirt from it. She desperately searched for a woodland pool to wash it in – but they never seemed to be around anymore.

For years life went on in this way for Cinderella – working, giving, moving, giving, wondering, wandering, giving what she could. Some people were happier for having known her, or even having just crossed paths with her (though of course there were always the people who just wanted her to mind her own business).

Still, she searched. She sought. Her life became one of vague dissatisfactions mixed with moments of profound meaning and great beauty.

More years passed. Cinderella now felt that her name no longer suited her. It suggested youth and castles and things that were no longer a part of her life. "Cindy" also sounded too youngish, "Rella" was ridiculous. So she chose the middle and ambiguous letters of her name, "Dere" (pronouncing it Deera). The name suited her quite well, having no meaning attached to it whatsoever.

Another ten years went by and Dere's knees began to ache, especially when climbing stairs. "Good thing I gave up being a maid servant – my knees would not have withstood the floor scrubbing."

At night, she sometimes awoke from her sleep and thought – As much as I love some of my things and some of the moments in some of my days, I need more. Why is it that I still don't know what it is?

These sudden dark moments in the middle of the night were becoming more and more frequent. *What if it just gets worse?*

Oh, stop with the dark thoughts, she told herself. You know this occasionally happens in the heart of the night – just fill your mind with your beautiful things. Take ten deep breaths and on each breath weave it with a dream image. And soon she was asleep, dreaming of polar bears, of all things. Sometimes the imaging didn't work as planned.

(*"Whoa!"* said Nora. *"This story's all over the place."* Honey gave a little shrug. *"It always has been."*)

One day, Dere went to her trunk in the attic of her house, and sifted through the layers of memories until she came upon a blue dress she had made many years ago – so like the one she had worn to the ball once upon a time. It was still beautiful, still full of promise and excitement.

Dere, in front of the old standing mirror that stands in all fictional attics, tried on the old dress – but she couldn't get it over her hips. *Huh – it must have shrunk.*

Off came the dress. But when she tucked it back into the trunk, she saw the old rose and green and gold shawl. She lifted it, shook it open, and draped it around her shoulders. It still fit.

Sitting on the trunk, shawl wrapped around her, she looked into the mirror and saw her young self, layered over by her old self and wondered: *What is it all for? How, now, can I find meaning? What dream will I now follow? For what is life without a dream?*

She got out a pencil and a pad of paper and listed all her dreams. Romantic love, family, dear friends. Truth and beauty, wealth, or at least material comfort. To see the beautiful places and faraway cities of the world, to know and be a part of the excitement and magnificence of life. Throughout the years she had found only bits and pieces of her various dreams. Maybe there was no reaching the dream, and the dream was simply the way you decided to live each day, making the most of life's path.

Another glance in the mirror. *Maybe yoga? Maybe I should repaint the house? Is this midlife crisis again? When does it become post-midlife crisis? When do you get old enough that this longing and dissatisfaction ceases to be a crisis? And you realize that this is just life, deal with it.*

She thought about that magical night at the palace and the gossamer blue dress that turned into air. And then chided herself: *Forget about the dress, forget about those uncomfortable shoes! If it's transformation you're after, how about some travel?*

Righto! I'm not giving up, I'm not giving in. Dere adjusted the shawl around her shoulders in a rather dramatic fashion, held her head high, and descended the attic stairs, the second-floor stairs, and the stairs out the front door. "I'm getting rather good at these embarkations to new destinations, new paths."

Let the journey continue, let the adventure begin, let the dream expand into some new glorious direction! Suddenly, the sky seemed a richer shade of blue, the leaves of the trees a more vibrant green, the air fragrant with delicate scents of new spring growth – except that it was the middle of a rainy wintry day.

Yes, why not? With a smile of triumph and excitement she walked down the sidewalk, and then paused and thought – perhaps I should pack this time. Perhaps I should make some kind of a plan.

The neighbors shook their heads as they observed her and thought she was becoming even more eccentric. Where was she going with just a shawl on? What did she look so happy about?

Dere turned around and went back up the stairs. She went into the house and built a fire in her cozy fireplace. It *was* a rather cold day to begin a new journey. She made herself a cup of tea and looked out the window at the rain that was turning into snow. *Dreams, dreams,* she thought, *please bloom in me, and let me bloom in you. I will make this room, this moment, this cup of tea, part of the dream.* And she smiled contentedly.

Years passed in which several trips were taken, many wishes were granted, and plans were made.

On mild days, she sat out in her beloved garden and continued to dream her beautiful dreams.

On such future-filled afternoons, with the breeze blowing her gray hair and fluttering her shawl, her "list of extraordinary things to do" resting on her lap, Dere would smile out at her garden and up at the sky, and wonder at the sweet wonder of the world.

THE END

Honora leaned back and scrutinized the finality of those closing two words. She looked at Nora, and over at Honey. Then she crossed out THE END and wrote THE BEGINNING.

Honora smiled. Honey and Nora smiled. Honora knew that she herself must be well into Act IV of her play, nearing the end of her story. And yet – she felt so young sometimes. So full of all she still wanted to do, be, see, feel, write!

As a matter of fact, Honora was more than ready to begin a new adventure. *What about a climb to Machu Picchu – I hear there's a train that gets you most of the way there? Or brush up on my Spanish and spend some time in Pamplona. Attempt to learn French again? How about Italian? Let's go wider – how about Hindi? Sketch the Taj Mahal. Why not?* Honora smiled as she looked out the window. *Ah, the world, the world!*

The Old Cobbler, Natasha, Cinderella, the Fairy Godmother, and the rest – they all agreed. There is still time, there is always time. If you can think that thought, then that means there is still time. Time to live, time to enrich another life, time to create another chapter in your life's story! Age of spirit is all that matters, and Honora/Nora/ Honey was still full of zest for life. In fact, she felt like she was just warming up. Perhaps she was just getting started.

Honora leaned back in her chair and thought:

How delightful! To reach the end, only to discover that it's another beginning!

And what better way to mark a new beginning than with a new Notebook! (Nora beamed at the use of three! exclamation points. Honey was already mentally packing her favorite clothes.)

Honora brought the new notebook to her table and took the cap off her pen. She sat up tall, opened the first page, and smoothed the blank sheet.

She inhaled deeply, blew out a chestful of air, and smiled. Then with a flourish she wrote:

Book the Fourth

Now then, I take pen in hand and write . . .

CPSIA information can be obtained
at www.ICGtesting.com
Printed in the USA
BVHW091226011122
650797BV00002B/11